TALES OF LOVE AND MYSTERY

James Hogg

This portrait of James Hogg appeared in The Mirror of Literature, Amusement, and Instruction, *a London two-penny magazine, in January 1833. Reproduced courtesy of the Trustees of the National Library of Scotland.*

TALES
OF LOVE
AND MYSTERY

JAMES HOGG

edited by David Groves

CANONGATE

1985

First published in 1985
by Canongate Publishing Limited
17 Jeffrey Street, Edinburgh

*The publishers acknowledge the financial assistance
of the Scottish Arts Council in the
publication of this volume*

British Library Cataloguing in Publication Data

Hogg, James, *1770-1835*
Tales of love and mystery
I. Title   II. Groves, David
823′.7[F]   PR4791.A4

ISBN 0-86241-085-1
ISBN 0-86241-103-3 Pbk

Typeset by Witwell Limited, Liverpool
Printed and bound by Clark Constable, Edinburgh

CONTENTS

INTRODUCTION

Byron, travelling in Italy in 1820, received a parcel containing two books of *Winter Evening Tales* written by his friend James Hogg. He read them avidly, and declared that they were 'rough but *racy* — and welcome.'[1] As a writer of stories and poems James Hogg was highly regarded in his own time, with admirers who included Wordsworth, Walter Scott, John Galt, Washington Irving, the Brontës, and, almost certainly, Edgar Allan Poe. Other friends included the painters David Wilkie, William Allan, and the Naesmiths. Many editions of his tales appeared in Edinburgh, Glasgow, London, Newcastle, Paris and Berlin, and New York, Philadelphia, and Connecticut. But unfortunately Hogg's literary reputation has never recovered from the blanket of snobbery and prudishness cast over it by nineteenth-century editors after his death.

James Hogg was born in Ettrick Forest, in the south of Scotland, in 1770. His parents were tenant-farmers who soon lost their land and money in a depression. Young Jamie received less than half-a-year of schooling. From the age of seven until he was almost forty, he worked as a cowherd, shepherd, or farmer in the Borders of Scotland. At fifteen he 'saved five shillings of my wages, with which I bought an old violin. This occupied all my leisure hours, and has been my favourite amusement ever since.' The young shepherd would practise for an hour or two each evening, 'sawing over my favourite old Scottish tunes' alone in the barn or stable where he slept. By his twenties James Hogg was a popular fiddler at weddings and local country dances. His love of music led him to try writing songs, then poems, and eventually stories and novels.

The shepherd composed his earliest pieces while sitting in a field surrounded by his flock and his sheep-dog Sirrah. 'I had no more difficulty in composing songs then than I have at present,' he tells us in 1832,

> and I was equally well pleased with them. But ... though I always stripped myself of coat and vest when I began to pen a song, yet my wrist took a cramp, so that I could rarely make above four or six lines at a sitting ... Having very little spare time from my flock, which was unruly enough, I folded and stitched a few sheets of paper, which I carried in my pocket. I had no inkhorn; but, in place of it, I borrowed a small vial, which I fixed in a hole in the breast of my waistcoat; and having a cork fastened by a piece of twine, it answered the purpose fully as well. Thus equipped, whenever a leisure minute or two offered, and I had nothing else to do, I sat down and wrote out my thoughts as I found them. This is still my invariable practice in writing prose. I cannot make out one sentence by study, without the pen in my hand to catch the ideas as they arise, and I never write two copies of the same thing.

Hogg makes a clear distinction between his spontaneous method of writing 'songs' and 'prose', as described above, and his more painstaking practice in inventing poetry:

> My manner of composing poetry is very different,

and, I believe, much more singular. Let the piece be of what length it will, I compose and correct it wholly in my mind, or on a slate, ere ever I put pen to paper; and then I write it down as fast as the A, B, C. When once it is written, it remains in that state; it being, as you very well know, with the utmost difficulty that I can be brought to alter one syllable.[2]

Throughout his life James Hogg would repeat his claim of being an inspired writer, a man of genius whose work was virtually spontaneous and unrevised. His apparently unshakeable belief in the 'fire and rapidity of true genius'[3] made him impatient of criticism, and helps to explain both his frequent association of creativity with motion and speed, and his lifelong interest in writing about various kinds of journey. In the present collection of tales, 'Eastern Apologues' and 'Seeking the Houdy' both use either freedom of movement or the journey as metaphors for artistic creativity. Similarly, his famous satirical novel *The Private Memoirs and Confessions of a Justified Sinner* balances two narrators (the editor, writing in 1824, and Robert Wringhim, writing in 1712), each of whom embarks on a confused, embittering journey symbolising the error, the increasing uncertainty, and ultimately (at the end of their parallel journeys) the futility and loss of inspiration suffered by the two writers.[4] Writing is a process, according to Hogg, a 'mental journey' in which the mind is 'put in motion and displayed.' When an author 'is animated by the fire of nature, and his mind brought to its full tone of exertion, ... he will write more consistently with the rules of common sense, than if fettered by the best rules that ever reviewer laid down.'[5] His depictions of motion and journey allowed Hogg, at times, to live up to his own ideal of inspired 'genius,' since they provided a vehicle for directly expressing the creative process as he experienced it.

In fact James Hogg often revised his poems and stories. From time to time he concedes this point, writing to one publisher, for example, 'I have for many years been collecting the rural and traditionary tales of Scotland, and ... writing them over again, and new-modelling them.'[6] Nevertheless the notion of spontaneous imagination always remained important to Hogg. 'It is not necessary to have one head to invent and another to censure and correct,' he explains, 'for, certainly, the imagination which sketches the outlines is the best qualified to finish the picture.'[7]

During his thirties Hogg published many poems under his pseudonym of 'the Ettrick Sphepherd.' He also brought out accounts of his Highland Tours, and a book of advice for sheep-farmers. Although he would gladly have remained a shepherd or farmer all his life, an economic depression once again forced him to change course.

I found myself without employment, and without money, in my native country; therefore, in February 1810, in utter desperation, I took my plaid about my shoulders, and marched away to Edinburgh, determined, since no better could be, to push my fortune as a literary man. It is true, I had estimated my poetical talent high enough, but I had resolved to use it only as a staff, never as a crutch; and would have kept that resolve, had I not been driven to the reverse.[8]

His idea was to publish a weekly literary magazine in the capital. *The Spy* appeared in September 1810, began well, but ran aground after one year. The problem was that Hogg offended many subscribers with bawdy stories like the first version of his 'Love Adventures of Mr George Cochrane.' In the opinion of one reader, '*a more shameful and indecent paper was never laid so barefacedly before the public.*'[9] James Hogg should remain with the innocent 'brightest ideals of a poet's fancy,' said the reviewers, rather than venturing into his 'coarse, vulgar' style of prose, where he seemed only too likely to come 'into contact with the bodily animals of this sluggish earth.'[10]

Luckily Hogg paid little attention to the strictures of fashionable critics. In the last issue of *The Spy* he vents a healthy distrust of the genteel values he encountered in respectable, literary Edinburgh:

> The learned, the enlightened, and polite circles of this flourishing metropolis, disdained either to be amused or instructed by the ebulitions of humble genius. Enemies, swelling with the most rancorous spite, grunted in every corner; ... pretended friends ... liberal in their advices ... took every method in their power to lessen the work in the esteem of others, by branding its author with designs the most subversive of all civility and decorum.[11]

A decade later at the age of forty-nine, the Ettrick Shepherd married. He and his wife Margaret had five children, and lived happily in rural Lowland Scotland until Hogg's death at sixty-four. During these years his greatest work appeared, with his *Confessions of a Justified Sinner* coming out in 1824. James Hogg was a warm, generous man, with many friends; he leaves us with this picture of himself, in his last years, at an evening party in Edinburgh:

> Then, with 'O, I beg your pardon, Hogg, I was forgetting,' [the host, Mr Sym] would take out a small gold key ... and stalk away as tall as the life, open two splendid fiddle cases, and produce their contents, first the one, and then the other; but always keeping the best to himself ... Then down we sat side by side, and began — at first gently, and with easy motion, like skilful grooms, keeping ourselves up for the final heat, which was slowly but surely approaching. At the end of every tune we took a glass, and still our enthusiastic admiration of the Scottish tunes increased — our energies of execution redoubled, till, ultimately, it became not only a complete and well-contested race, but a trial of strength to determine which should drown the other. The only feelings short of ecstasy, that came across us in these enraptured moments, were caused by hearing the laugh and joke going on with our friends, as if no such thrilling strains had been flowing.[12]

Yet Hogg's peasant origins, his lack of formal education, and his 'full-blooded response to life'[13] made powerful enemies on every side. An audience that wanted its authors to be polite, circumspect, and obedient, was not likely to appreciate the directness, spontaneity, and bold simplicity of Hogg's fiction and poetry. One very respectable and reverend critic announced that the Shepherd was 'grotesque,' 'raised far above his proper sphere,' and 'a wretched clown, unworthy of the smallest consideration, except as a butt for ridicule or derision.'[14] The same snobbish prejudices can be heard in this contrast between Hogg and his elegant Edinburgh booksellers:

> Only picture to yourself a stout country lout, with a bushel of hair on his shoulders that had not been raked for months, enveloped in a coarse plaid impregnated with tobacco, with a prodigious mouthful of immeasurable tusks, and a dialect that set all conjecture at defiance, lumbering suddenly in upon the elegant retirement of Mr Miller's backshop, or the dim seclusion of Mr John Ogle! Were these worthies to be blamed if they fainted upon the spot, or run out yelling into the street past the monster ...?[15]

Unlike his detractors, James Hogg never pretends, in his writing, to possess absolute, final values, or to be able to judge other people with absolute certainty. A deep sense of the mysteriousness of human life is one of his distinguishing qualities as an author: whether depicting love, dreams, the supernatural, historical events, or suffering or cruelty, he almost always begins by leading his characters down into a realm of profound confusion where normal values, identities, and expectations dissolve. To many of his contemporaries, chaos was something to be studiously avoided, but for Hogg the chaos is an unavoidable condition of life, a state which must be confronted honestly and endured courageously if deliverance is to be found. The Shepherd's freedom from false sophistication, snobbery, and intellectual pride enables him to win through to universal values, and to find a sense of 'myth' or process in life. It is this simple wisdom that, in his stories and poems, he repeatedly finds new ways of re-creating.

'The Mistakes of a Night'

James Hogg was twenty-three when his first work appeared anonymously in *The Scots Magazine*. 'The Mistakes of a Night' is set in Ettrick and Yarrow, where Hogg lived most of his life, and mentions Robert Cramond, a local minister. Apparently the editor of the magazine had doubts about publishing the poem, for he explains that he only wanted 'to encourage a young poet,' adding rather pompously that Hogg should 'be at more pains to make his rhymes answer, and ... attend more to grammatical accuracy.'

Yet despite some naiveté 'The Mistakes of a Night' contains the embryo of James Hogg's greatest work. It is the first of his many depictions of a loving, encouraging mother-figure, together with the decidedly ambivalent response she evokes from the young man. The poem has a slightly Chekhovian tone in the way it appeals on two distinct levels, with a comic surface and an undertone of darker psychological insight.

Geordie's 'Mistakes' are not the only kind of confusion, in this tale. The poet is uncertain whether to write in English or Scots, and frequently slips from one language to the other. He also maintains a delicate balance between arousing the sexual passions of his readers, and trying to obey conventional morality. Internal contradictions like these abound in the early writings of James Hogg; far from being a limitation, however, they are the impetus that will eventually bring him to forge what I call his 'myth' of a descent into confusion which leads finally to a discovery of community, fellowship, and clarity.

'Singular Dream'

This story first appeared in 1811 under the title 'Evil Speaking Ridiculed by an Allegorical Dream' in Hogg's periodical *The Spy*, where it takes the form of a letter to the editor. Evidence suggests that the Shepherd's friend and advisor James Gray helped him with the first draft. A revised version, under the improved title, appeared nine years later in the *Winter Evening Tales*.

As well as being one of his best and funniest pieces, 'Singular Dream' illustrates in full the 'myth' or meaningful sequence that is basic to Hogg's work. It is a forerunner of the *Confessions of a Justified Sinner* in its economical treatment of demonic possession, the *doppelganger* or double, and dissolving or merging personal identities. Hogg builds slowly to a comic climax by stressing the contrast between the caustic Mr A.T., and the fussy, earnest, well-intentioned, and ludicrously gullible narrator. He then takes us into the narrator's dream-world, where absurdly the dreamer assumes a heroic stance that he sadly lacks in reality. The dreamer hopes to save mankind, but he ends up (a little like Geordie in 'The Mistakes of a Night') 'entangled among women and petticoats.'

Like many of Hogg's stories, 'Singular Dream' traces a main character's loss of innocence, his initiation into corruption, chaos, and extreme confusion, and in the end his discovery of a higher innocence. The narrator

first encounters corruption through the remarks of Mr
A.T., after which he falls into a murky dream-world of
shifting identities, where the minister can turn into
Satan, then into a pig, and finally into Mr A.T. himself.
After awakening, the narrator realises that by
'assenting implicitly' to A.T.'s slanders, he too had
momentarily become a 'limb or agent' in this demonic
chain of melting personal identities.

In his dream the narrator confronts, on a frightening,
primitive level, the relativity and fragility of the self. He
awakens and vows to implement that knowledge, on a
higher, conscious, and civilised level, by giving up
selfish pretensions of superiority in favour of
community and 'a higher opinion of the dignity of
human nature.'

The theme of 'Singular Dream' is the unity of
mankind, and the folly of individual pride. Those who
deny human fellowship jeopardise their own personal
identity, like Mr A.T., who, according to the logic of
the dream, becomes a split personality whose nature
shifts from the human to the animal to the demonic.
The narrator, likewise, temporarily loses his normal
selfhood, to become merely a 'limb . . . of the devil' until
he returns to a less proud and more generous
perspective, one which stresses humility, friendship,
and love. The dream is indeed 'Singular' because it
conveys the essential oneness of people.

At the end of 'Singular Dream' Hogg uses a
favourite ploy by suddenly placing the whole story in a
new context. We now find that the narrator's letter has
been an elaborate defence against a charge of assault laid
by Mr A.T. From this newer perspective the tale
becomes a rather far-fetched vindication by the

accused, especially when we recall his pointed comment that his adversary Mr A.T. had denounced the judges of Edinburgh as 'a set of gossiping, gormandizing puppies ... fast bringing the city to ruin.' The wry inventiveness of the ending invites us to read 'Singular Dream' once again, working out its ironic implications from a more comic perspective. As in almost every one of James Hogg's stories, no single character is allowed a monopoly on objective truth.

'Love Adventures of Mr George Cochrane'

A first instalment of this novella was published in Hogg's weekly *Spy*, where its lusty qualities contributed to the quick decline of that periodical. The story illustrates what one critic called 'that coarse and libidinous vulgarity in which the Shepherd revels as in his native element.'[16]

In 1820 the complete 'Love Adventures' appeared in Hogg's collection of *Winter Evening Tales*. Many readers were offended, but others felt that this nimble account of 'the days o' warstling an' wooing' was 'by far the best of the Tales.' A critic in *Blackwood's Magazine* found the style 'so perfectly natural, unaffected, and unelaborate ... that we have considered ourselves all along as listening to our worthy friend's own conversation, rather than as reading a book of his writing.' This reviewer goes on to recall hearing Hogg tell similar stories 'in nearly the same words,' but

as having befallen no less a person than the Ettrick Shepherd himself. He has, no doubt, good reasons for not *now* [that is, since his recent marriage] wishing to represent himself as an actor in some of the scenes ... and, moreover, it is not impossible that his own personal share in them was, after all, no better than an embellishment, devised for the purpose of making us listen to them with more zest than we might otherwise have done, over our sober bowl at Young's or Ambrose's [Taverns].[17]

Hogg himself always claimed that 'Those who desire to peruse my youthful love adventures will find some of the best of them in those of "George Cochrane." '[18] On the other hand, Cochrane is clearly a fictional creation, an ironic, many-sided character who is *un*like James Hogg in his spurious sentimentalism, his alienation from Border society, and his mercenary, lazy, and Anglicised ways.

Whether or not the 'Love Adventures' are autobiographical, they paint an intriguing, authentic picture of rural life in the south of Scotland, and accurately reflect ancient traditions of love-making. A journalist of the time tells us that

in the course of his passion, a Scottish peasant often exerts a spirit of adventure, of which a Spanish cavalier need not be ashamed. After the labours of the day are over, he sets out for the habitation of his mistress, perhaps at many miles distance, regardless of the length or dreariness of the way. He approaches her in secrecy, under the disguise of night. A signal at the door or window, perhaps agreed on, and understood by none but her, gives information of his arrival, and sometimes it is repeated again and again, before the capricious fair one will obey the summons. But if she favours his addresses, she escapes [from the house] unobserved, and receives the vows of her lover under the gloom of twilight, or the deeper shade of night.

'Interviews of this kind' were so common, in the words of this reporter, that 'the embers of passion' were 'continually fanned' in Scotland, 'to a degree ... seldom found ... in other countries.' As a result 'the clergy and elders' found it necessary to 'exercise their zeal,' handing out punishments to sexual culprits in the form of a 'public rebuke from the pulpit, for three sabbaths successively, in the face of the congregation.'[19] There is evidence that James Hogg himself may have fathered at least one illegitimate child, and, according to one report he was required to mount 'the repenting-stool' in 1814 at his local church:

The bonny, blooming, little ewe-milker, whose charms had caused James to deflect from the path of moral rectitude, stood at his elbow, ... suffused with scarlet blushes, such as dimmed even the splendour of her accomplice's whiskers. He, meantime, maintained a stern, dogged, sullen obduracy ... and when all the horrors of holy rhetoric were at length exhausted, ... nimbly and gaily did Jamie hop from his pedestal, and was received almost with plaudits among a goodly company of brother-swains, who had [come to the church] rather to do him honour than to witness his humiliation. At the kirk door Hogg drew the ewe-milker under his arm, and away the two glided together, with apparently as much *sang froid* as if nothing particular had happened.[20]

It is not surprising that the 'Love Adventures of Mr George Cochrane' caused some offence among Hogg's first readers. 'The sea, to be sure, is very deep,' an eager mistress informs George, 'but he is a great coward who dares not wade to the knee in it!" The hero recounts his adventures in 'night courting,' and gleefully informs his 'Edinburgh readers' that 'every young woman in the country must be courted at night, or else they will not be courted at all.' Yet although George claims to have 'never ... met with an unfavourable reception,' we soon see that he is a very frustrated and confused person, repeatedly the victim of women who resent his cavalier assumptions of male dominance. As each of his five relationships comes to an end, he slowly learns to value an ideal of harmony, unity, and fellowship, at the same time as he confronts the reality of distrust between the sexes, between the opposing factions of Scottish society, and above all within his own mind.

Youthful experiences may have given Hogg the raw materials, but as a work of art his 'Love Adventures' attains thematic unity through suggestive nuances and an appropriate structure. It takes a survey of Scottish society by presenting George in amorous affairs with five different women: the first is a servant girl and the second a woman of 'elevated rank,' while the third is a Catholic, the fourth a Cameronian (or extreme Presbyterian), and the fifth a fairly moderate (but excessively pious and, alas, middle-aged) Presbyterian. The contrasts between these successive lovers, together with the implied desirability of marriage, emphasise Hogg's theme of the need for a more unified nation.

George Cochrane falls from favour with his third mistress, the Catholic Mary, when he arrives for a lover's tryste twenty-four hours too late, having misunderstood her use of the word 'eve.'

'Are you so childishly ignorant,' returned she, 'as not to know that the eve of a festival, holiday, or any particular day whatever, always precedes the day nominally?' I denied the position positively, in all its parts and bearings ...

'Never tell me of your old Popish saws and customs; the whole of your position is founded in absurdity, my love,' said I ...

'I could go farther back, and to higher authority, than old Popish saws, as you call them, for the establishment of my position, if I chose,' said she; 'I could take the account of the first formation of the day and the night, where you will find it recorded, that "the *evening* and the morning were the first day"...'

'Nothing can be more plain,' said I, 'than that the evening of a day is the evening of that day.'

'Nothing can,' said she.

'And, moreover,' said I, 'has not the matter been argued thoroughly by our christian divines?'

'It has,' said she.

Comic dialogues like this quietly sketch in the social and theological background to George's adventures, and suggest a parallel between the two highly imperfect kinds of human love, sexual and religious. Love quickly sours to enmity, in the cultural milieu of this story.

George's next lover is Jessy, the daughter of Cameronian parents. Like Mary, Jessy has a taste for contention, but in a more physical form — she sets up wrestling competitions among her lovers. This fourth relationship neatly contrasts with the preceding one, and again evokes the religious schisms that have vitiated Scottish society. When George prepares to stay the night with Jessy, the puritanical mother mutters suspiciously to her daughter, 'a cast o' grace thou'lt never get'; Jessy answers pertly that she hopes to receive 'a cast o' grace' that very evening. In his 'Love Adventures of Mr George Cochrane' Hogg often uses daring puns such as this one to juxtapose the spiritual and physical aspects of human love.

The relationships with Mary and Jessy, then, have undertones which hint at the Ettrick Shepherd's distrust of the two extremes in religion, and in his society as a whole. Through unobtrusive parallels between the two contrasting love affairs, he imparts his own commitment to a more authentic outlook which would be less dogmatic and divisive, and more natural. As in 'Singular Dream,' Hogg conveys his ideal of unity, and his awareness of disunity.

Finally, 'Love Adventures' makes an innovative use of conventional literary structure. 'The traditional structure of comedy,' as Northrop Frye reminds us, 'is one which leads up to the birth of a new society, usually crystallizing around the marriage of the hero and heroine, in the conventional "happy ending" of the final scene.'[21] The comic tone of Hogg's novella, and its subject-matter, would lead readers to expect a traditional (comic) marriage at the end, but instead George merely becomes an old bachelor, bemoaning the fact that he never married. James Hogg breaks the conventional literary mould, to indicate that no unity is achieved, and no new society is born, in the divided Scotland of his 'Love Adventures.'

'Eastern Apologues'

Didactic moral fables like Dr Johnson's *Rasselas* or
Voltaire's *Candide* were popular during the eighteenth
century and after. It was partly in the spirit of this
tradition that Hogg wrote his 'Eastern Apologues' in
1829 for a Christmas Annual called *Forget Me Not*.
Fortunately his fable is livelier than most, and it
approaches comedy through shafts of irony and
through obvious exaggeration in the figure of the too-
earnest Ismael, a 'mutilated man of mirth' who might
almost be seen as an ancestor of Beckett's Unnameable.
Although Hogg follows Dr Johnson in preaching the
virtue of contentment, he differs from most writers in
this genre by implying that real contentment is gained
through activity and motion, rather than by attaining
the stasis of ultimate wisdom.

'Eastern Apologues' may also be read as a satirical
allegory of Hogg's volatile relations with his embattled
Edinburgh publisher William Blackwood. Ismael
represents the Ettrick Shepherd, according to this
interpretation, and Sadac's servants represent
Blackwood's underlings — and especially his editors
John Wilson and J.G. Lockhart, with whom the
Shepherd kept up an uneasy friendship. Among
Hogg's previous efforts in this vein is the 'Ancient
Chaldee Manuscript,' which in 1817 caused a great
scandal by mocking Edinburgh's literary worthies in
Old Testament language.

Ismael's story of the goat and the ox is a clear
statement of one of Hogg's fundamental themes.
Rolling in the 'labyrinths of luxury,' the fat ox finds
that his obesity makes him a prisoner within the town

walls, whereas the wild goat enjoys the freedom of both town and country, like James Hogg himself. The happy goat, with his energy and freedom of motion, has also developed an ability to adjust and to cope with change, which helps him survive difficult times, in contrast to the 'unwieldy ox.' Although only a simple story, 'Eastern Apologues' illuminates Hogg's conception of art and his use of the journey motif in more ambitious works such as 'Seeking the Houdy' and the *Confessions of a Justified Sinner*.

While Ismael is partly a spokesman for the author, he too becomes a victim of Hogg's irony in the final pages, as the tables are turned and Sadac gets to instruct his friend in the 'rules of life.' Ismael represents the free imagination and 'the soul of man,' but Sadac (despite being morally corrupt) has at least the practical, necessary, and complementary wisdom of social perspective.

'Eastern Apologues' finds a compromise between the innocence of imagination, and the experience of social realities. Apparently both sides are necessary to human life. The retrospective qualification, the balanced irony, the real tension between opposing points of view, and the refusal to let any one character represent ultimate truth, are hallmarks of James Hogg's maturest writing.

'The First Sermon'

This, one of Hogg's finest poems, first appeared in *Blackwood's Magazine* in June 1830. 'The First Sermon' combines dramatic excellence, poised irony, and a crucial encounter with nothingness. It is also

convincingly set in its own time and place, with glances
at George Combe and the Edinburgh craze for
phrenology, Edmund Kean the actor, and fashionable
authors like Edinburgh's Hugh and Robert Blair and
preachers Logan, Gillespie, and Thomson.

As in the *Confessions of a Justified Sinner*, 'The First
Sermon' combines a religious protagonist with a more
rational-minded commentator or narrator. But despite
their differences we soon find that both men in the
poem are self-centred, self-righteous, and unable to
appreciate perspectives different from their own.
Shallow, mechanical, and arrogant, the narrator is a
perfect counterpart to the narrow and self-glorifying
preacher.

Believing that God will put the words in his mouth,
the naive young puritan preacher tries to give a
spontaneous sermon. He soon loses the thread of his
argument, and then loses all presence of mind and
stumbles abruptly on an agonising vision of
nothingness, as

all within
Became a blank — a chaos of confusion,
Producing nought but agony of soul.

The clergyman's discovery of the void, the 'vacancy
within,' resembles similar discoveries by twentieth-
century thinkers: 'Man is all the time outside of
himself,' as Sartre puts it. A human being 'is not
definable ... because to begin with he is nothing.'[22]

Unlike the rest of the congregation, the narrator has
a good laugh over the young man's discomfiture, and
then retires to a full dinner. The narrator, as we slowly
come to understand, is callow, pompous, Anglicised,

and incapable of comprehending the misfortune of his fellow-countryman. His credibility is further undermined by the tragic ending of the poem, which suddenly casts a more human light on the would-be minister. Completely underestimating the story he is reporting, the narrator simply concludes with a recipe for avoiding any future 'outrageous scene' like the one he has witnessed. He sees the 'ordeal' as merely social, a failure in polite conduct, rather than an agony with spiritual, tragic, or existential implications. Even the narrator's kindness is a delusion; he wants to help 'young beginners' by obliterating the void, by smothering it over with a 'snug opening of the blessed book.'

Neither the preacher nor the narrator understands or even questions his own motives. The one tries to be a passive mouthpiece of God, and the other never rises above commonplace snobbish judgments concerning what 'One scarcely can approve.' In spite of their contrasting ideologies, each man defines himself by making a rapid retreat from the void, either through suicide or by hiding behind fatuous judgments of what 'I have oft bethought me it were best.' They are equidistant from the author himself, whose more complicated attitude towards religion can be found in his *Brownie of Bodsbeck*, 'Scottish Psalmody Defended,' and *Lay Sermons*.

Compared with 'The Mistakes of a Night' thirty-six years earlier, 'The First Sermon' indicates a tremendous growth in James Hogg's ability to focus on a difficult theme through irony, imagery, structure, and a careful, dramatic control of voice. His main personal concern is still the descent into confusion, but he is now able to convey that theme with clarity and balance.

'Seeking the Houdy'

This story (which takes place near Meggat Water, just west of the Borders) appeared in 1830 in the London *Forget Me Not*, a fashionable literary Annual for women. Much of its humour derives from the hero's subservience and frustration in a world controlled, apparently, by women. Life is shaped and directed entirely, in this tale, by the feminine principle: Robin is an ineffectual man surrounded by women, his wife gives birth to a daughter, his mare refuses to co-operate with him and resents being separated from her foal, and Robin himself has been sent by his wife in search of a mid-wife, or 'houdy.' After being ridden by a witch, the hero is found, unconscious and naked, by the old wives of the village, who then bathe him and ply him with embarrassing questions. The dream-like, womb-like atmosphere adds to the impression of a world dominated by women.

'Seeking the Houdy' is a clever metaphor for Hogg's predicament as a writer trying to appeal to the respectable women readers of the *Forget Me Not*. As one critic explained in the *Court and Fashionable Magazine*, the Annuals were elegant books richly bound in 'unwonted splendour of attire' and lavishly illustrated with engraved 'embellishments.' In their rarified tales and dainty samples of the 'poetical *morceau*,' the Annuals permitted 'nothing injurious in example or sentiment.'[23] The Ettrick Shepherd of course felt deeply alienated from the literary fashions that prevailed among well to do people of his time. He once wrote to the editor of *Forget Me Not*, protesting against 'the rage for Annuals' and declaring that 'such vapid lady stuff must pall the public'.[24] It seems likely, then, that Hogg was well aware of obvious similarities between the situation of the hero in 'Seeking the Houdy,' and his own situation in writing for the Annuals.

The first half of this story is told in a fairly artificial, Anglicised, genteel style, which captures the spirit of the Annuals and also reflects the slowness of Robin and his horse. But the second half is mainly in Scots vernacular, which brings tremendous vitality and corresponds to the horse's sudden speed, once the witch has climbed onto its back behind Robin. Like the 'Love Adventures of Mr George Cochrane' and the *Confessions of a Justified Sinner*, 'Seeking the Houdy' contains suggestive parallels between its different parts, and tries to provoke the reader into analysing the points of difference.

The two main parts of this tale represent reason and instinct, respectively. In the first half Robin thinks it 'the most natural and reasonable thing in the world' that his mare should obey his commands, while she, on the contrary, is 'inwardly convinced that the most natural and reasonable path she could take was the one straight home again to her foal.' The battle between man and horse becomes a kind of mock-debate, and the reader feels, like Robin, the inefficacy of reason.

Robin's complacent cruelty to his mare is another symptom of the deliberate one-sidedness of the first part of 'Seeking the Houdy,' and a sure sign of the author's ironic intent. Although a keen angler and fisher, Hogg vociferously opposed practices which imposed unnecessary suffering on animals. His essay 'On the Effects of Mole-Catching' argues against 'unnatural … persecutions' of pigeons, rooks, moles, and indeed 'any class of creatures with which the all-wise Creator of the universe has seen meet to stock a country.'[25] Through the relationship between Robin and his mare Hogg implies that intellect by itself is aggressive, tends to repress the animal side of human nature, and cannot achieve freedom, movement, or creativity.

If reason dominates the first half of the story, instinct dominates the second half, and Robin is equally helpless. He soon finds himself 'lootching forret' in the saddle, 'cleaving the wind like an arrow out of a bow.' The speed, the vitality, and the urgency of this section, together with its onomatopoeic qualities and its powerful images drawn from folklore and scripture, make an effective contrast to the inertia of the earlier part. Instinct plunges the rider headlong into a chaotic world 'like a confused dream.' Normal linear time does not exist in this realm, since the old woman Robin meets is also inexplicably his newborn daughter. Characteristically Hogg makes no attempt to explain the mystery. The reader is simply led down into an underworld, and left there. The chaos, confusion, and fear must be encountered on their own terms, rather than as things to be explained away through reason.

On one level 'Seeking the Houdy' is a statement about the creative process as James Hogg experienced it. As long as he tries to write in an English, genteel mode, Hogg's progress is as slow as Robin's when first setting out; but once he turns to the Scots language and local traditions, he finds himself propelled by an instinctive creative force over which he has little conscious control. Meanwhile, in this story, the real act of creativity (that is, the giving of birth by Robin's wife) takes place off-stage, and is even further removed from Robin's conscious efforts. Hogg identifies himself quite clearly with Robin the shepherd in the final paragraph, where he laments that 'those days are over' and that 'no future old shepherd shall tell another tale of SEEKING THE HOUDY.' The narrator's regret for the decay of 'midwifery, that primitive and original calling, in this primitive and original country,' recalls the Ettrick Shepherd's interest in preserving the primitive, original traditions of Scotland, and reminds us that the artist was nearing the end of his life. While his wife represents the hidden powers of the imagination, the houdy and Robin represent, respectively, the inspiration of folk wisdom and the (ineffectual) conscious ego. Robin's adventures with the houdy help us understand Hogg's life-long reluctance to alter what he had written with the 'fire and rapidity of true genius.'

'Some Terrible Letters from Scotland'

This spine-chilling tale appeared in April 1832 in *The Metropolitan*, a London magazine run by the Scottish expatriate Thomas Campbell. Hogg's successful visit to London during the first three months of 1832 is briefly mentioned in the opening sentence. The letters are based on a cholera epidemic which had swept through the slums and working-class areas of Britain the year before. While writing this story, Hogg might also have been recalling an incident from his days as a farmhand:

I had, from my childhood, been affected by the

frequent return of a violent inward complaint; and it attacked me once in a friend's house, at a distance from home, and, increasing to an inflammation, all hopes were given up of my recovery. While I was lying in the greatest agony, about the dead of night, I had the mortification of seeing the old woman, who watched over me, fall into a swoon, from a supposition that she saw my *wraith*: — a spirit which, the vulgar suppose, haunts the abodes of such as are instantly to die, in order to carry off the soul as soon as it is disengaged from the body: and, next morning, I overheard a consultation about borrowing sheets to lay me in at my decease.[26]

'Some Terrible Letters' establishes a mood of terror from the first sentence, with its reference to William Burke, a notorious Edinburgh murderer who sold his victims' corpses to medical men for dissection. Our horror deepens as we adjust to the plaintive, passive, defeated tone of the first letter-writer, and we experience a little of the despair of the terminally-ill. Andrew Ker's prosaic and matter-of-fact attitude only seems to envelop the reader in the increasing agony of death by cholera. As well as physical pain, Hogg also conveys the guilt that Andrew feels at being a cause of infection to those he loves.

The second letter is in several ways a contrast to the first. Alexander M'Alister writes in a detached, jocular tone that is likely to alienate most readers. Unlike Andrew, Alexander does not share in the suffering he describes, and he seems oblivious to the fact that he and his shipmates are probably responsible for spreading the infection.

The third letter is the best. It builds to a horrifying intensity, yet this movement is lightened by comic touches such as the picture of the Calvinistic busybody mother who takes great pleasure in running all day from one victim to another. Like M'Alister, she seems supremely unaware of her guilt in passing the cholera infection to those around her.

The mention of William Burke in the final sentence of 'Some Terrible Letters' echoes the beginning of the story, and challenges us to find a thematic unity underlying its three parts. Each of the letters combines grim naturalism with suggestions of the supernatural, and depicts physical illness in a way that draws both characters and readers into a world of confusion, terror, and evil. Traditional moral beliefs and categories seem irrelevant at this level of existence, since all people are equally guilty in the sense of being capable of spreading the infection. Hogg almost never attempts to answer the questions or soothe the anxieties that his stories arouse, yet in place of a panacea he at least finds a deep sense of human kinship through the stripping away of illusions and inessentials.

'Some Terrible Letters' shows human communities united by their subjection to natural forces, their apprehensions of the supernatural, and their mutual fear of infection from each other. As this tale presents them, human beings are essentially frightened, confused, suspicious, and helpless, without any real understanding of the source or cause of their suffering. Paradoxically it is their tragic isolation which implicitly unites people and provides the basis for James Hogg's vision of fellowship.

'Scottish Haymakers'

Three years before his death Hogg was asked for a story to accompany a lithograph of 'The Scottish Haymakers' in the *Forget Me Not*. The following spring he promised the editor to

> furnish you with something for the Haymakers if God spare me life and health. I was sorry I was obliged to break my word to you last year but it was the same with all other editors. My literary engagements are getting beyond my power to execute for always as I grow older and less qualified the demand on me is growing the greater.[27]

The story and the engraving appeared in print together by November.

No sign of declining powers or self-pity is evident in this engaging tale. Its theme is the relationship of art to life, which is appropriate, since Hogg is rendering a slightly fictionalised account of an episode in his own past, one which occurred sometime during the early 1820's. By simplifying the dialogue and reducing the number of characters, the author gives shape and meaning to a real event, as he quietly imparts equilibrium and a sense of more universal values. Two painters, a ventriloquist, the actor Daniel Terry, and three writers (Hogg, Scott, and John Grieve)[28] make up the party of seven artists, who are ranged against the seven labourers (four haymakers, the landlord, and his wife and daughter). It never seems to occur to most of the artists that Monsieur Alexandre's ventriloquism creates a great deal of extra work for the unfortunate labourers. But in contrast to their callous social superiors, the peasants show authentic concern when they believe that a baby is being smothered under the hay. They quickly unload, then re-load, their wagon, while the men of aesthetic sensibilities stand around watching idly. Even after 'Mr Scott and I' have 'stripped off our coats, and assisted,' the other artists merely continue enjoying the spectacle of hardworking haymakers. In the second half of the tale Monsieur Alexandre shows the same arrogance, amusing his friends by causing fear, destruction, and confusion at the inn. Alexandre's behaviour is remarkably like that of the demonic Gil-Martin in Hogg's *Confessions of a Justified Sinner*, and afterwards Hogg guesses that the workers are (quite understandably) 'never . . . so glad to get quit of a party in all their lives.'

Through the figure of Monsieur Alexandre Hogg is expressing his reservations about art and the aesthetic temperament. The story implies that artistic vision requires to be tempered with moral concern. Without that sense of responsibility, art can become empty, trivial, and divorced from its basis in real life.

'It is amazing how little makes a good picture,' says the painter Alexander Naesmith to James Hogg; 'and frequently the less that is taken in the better.' Hogg evidently took the advice to heart, and in this sketch he achieves profundity through simple, understated brushwork. The tensions between the seven artists and seven workers are cunningly developed, with a similar catastrophe occurring to one member of each group. Thus, Sandy Burnet, frightened by the ventriloquist's art, 'ran off, and never once looked over his shoulder,' living afterwards 'in a deranged state of mind,' while the artist Peter Naesmith, running a race with his father on the way home from the inn, falls, and receives a wound from which he eventually dies. The exact placing of the two disasters also invites us to look for parallels and contrasts between the two sections of 'Scottish Haymakers': Sandy runs away at the very end of the scene in the hayfield, while Peter runs away at the very end of the tavern scene. As in his 'Love Adventures,' 'First Sermon,' 'Seeking the Houdy,' 'Some Terrible Letters,' and other works, Hogg creates echoes and a careful balance to try to provoke his audience into analysing the theme and appreciating different points-of-view. The catastrophes which befall Sandy and Peter remind us that labourers and artists alike are human beings subject to a mysterious and often hostile universe.

'Though a perfect simpleton, he was a great man in his art.' These, the last words in 'Scottish Haymakers,' might serve as a description of James Hogg himself. Hogg never called attention to the clarity, precision, and perfect simplicity of his best tales; yet although these inconspicuous values are his greatest strength as a writer, they have also tended to encourage critics in drastically underestimating his importance. Even sympathetic readers have faulted Hogg with an 'aversion to deep thinking,' or complained that he 'rarely used his intellect with any profundity.'[29] These judgments unfortunately ignore both the considerable artistry and humane concern underlying his apparently 'ram-stam way of writing,'[30] and his ability to convey a love of life in imaginative, mythical terms, rather than primarily intellectual or abstract ones. The Shepherd was well aware that his work threatened prevailing attitudes in the urban, educated, genteel society of his day:

> For my own part, I know that I have always been looked on by the learned part of the community as an intruder in the paths of literature, and every opprobrium has been thrown on me from that quarter. The truth is, that I am so. The walks of learning are occupied by a powerful aristocracy, who deem that province their own peculiar right; else, what would avail all their dear-bought collegiate honours and degrees? No wonder that they should view an intruder, from the humble and despised ranks of the community, with a jealous and indignant eye, and impede his progress by every means in their power.[31]

James Hogg's hard-won simplicity, his freedom from false sophistication, snobbery, or intellectual pretension, is the key to his universality as a writer. His main personal theme is the discovery of extreme, irreducible mystery, which dissolves conventional values and identities, and which can only be overcome through the radical acceptance of human fellowship and oneness. Sometimes, as in 'Singular Dream,' he presents this basic 'myth' in full; his more common practice is to leave the reader at the lowest point of descent, and to challenge us through provocative, thoughtful ironies which hint at the possibility of deliverance.

Too many readers have known Hogg's work only through the dreadful bowdlerised editions produced by Victorian critics and clergymen. The present collection restores the original printed texts, with two exceptions, 'Singular Dream' and 'Love Adventures,' both of which are taken from the improved versions published by James Hogg in 1820 (rather than the incomplete or less subtle versions published earlier in *The Spy*). Of the eight pieces selected, none have been reprinted in the last hundred years, and all except three (— 'Singular Dream,' 'Love Adventures,' and 'The First Sermon' —) have until now only been available in rare surviving copies of the magazines or Annuals where they first appeared.

Obvious printing errors have been corrected in 'The Mistakes of a Night'. 'Astonied' has been changed to 'astonished' in one place in 'Eastern Apologues'. All other idiosyncrasies of grammar have been preserved. The footnotes with asterisks are ones that have been added for this edition.

A glossary is also provided. Most Scots expressions can easily be understood, however, if the reader will only listen to the sound, the context, or his or her own imagination.

I am grateful to Dr Douglas Mack for several helpful suggestions, and answers to my questions. Thanks are also due to Dr Ian Campbell in Edinburgh, Professor Brian Hepworth in Toronto, and to several members of the James Hogg Society: Gillian Hughes, Elaine Petrie, Barbara Bloedé, and Robin MacLachlan. A grant from the Social Sciences and Humanities Council of Canada allowed me to live in Scotland while preparing this selection. Finally, I would like to record my thanks to the courteous staff at the National Library of Scotland.

David Groves, Edinburgh, 1985

The Mistakes of a Night

TAK my advice, ye airy lads,
    That gang to see the lasses,
Keep weel your mind, for troth, the jads
    Tell ilka thing that passes.
Anither thing I wad advise,
    To gang on moon-light weather:
A friend o' mine, he was sae wise,
    He kiss't his lass's mither
                Ae Friday's Night.

She was a widow gaye an' douse,
    Liv'd o'er the hill frae Yarrow;
Her doughter Geordie lang had sought,
    And courtit for his marrow;
But 'twas in vain, she wadna do't
    Neither for gift nor fleechin;
Whilk sair provokit Geordie Scott,
    An' gart him flack the breechin,
                That Friday's night.

Awa' gaed Geordie hip and thigh,
    Out-o'er the muir to Maggy:
The night was neither warm nor dry,
    The road was rough an' haggy:
Wi' labour sair he reach'd the bit,
    By chance there stood her mither;
But Geordie ne'er observ'd the cheat,
    They spak sae sair like ither,
                That Friday's night.

He kiss't her o'er and o'er again,
   O'erjoy'd she was sae willin';
An' vow'd if she'd reject his flame,
   The very thought was killin'.
Then aff into the barn they hye,
   To spend the night in courtin';
The widow's heart did sing for joy,
   To think o' her good fortune,
              That Friday's night.

But when the cock began to cra',
   He left his saul's dear treasure,
And back the road he cam awa',
   He hugg'd himsel' wi' pleasure.
'The skittish elf was ay sae shy,
   'She fled whane'er I nam'd her:
'O! what a clever lad was I!
   'Faith, I trow I have tam'd her,
              'This lucky night.'

At length the widow proves nae right,
   Whilk soon as e'er she sa' man,
She gangs and tells the hail affair,
   To rev'rend Doctor C——d:
Geordie appears on his defence,
   Hears a' his accusation;
But, conscious of his innocence,
   He laughs at the relation
              O' Friday's night.

Says he, ' 'Tis false, this 'onest wife
   'May be a man for me, Sir!'
Quo' she, 'How dare ye, for your life
   'Attest so great a lie, Sir!'
Says he, 'If I a lie do tell,
   'To elders, priest, or bellman;
'Then may the miekle horned di'el,
   'Drive Geordie into hell, then,
              This very night.'

'I wish my lad,' quo' Elder Tam,
   'Ye wadna speak sae rashly,
'You've surely done this woman wrang,
   'Or else she ne'er wad fash ye.'
'Not I, Sir; I her ne'er did harm;
   'I never touch'd her skin yet:
'I own I kiss't her bonie bairn,
   'And hasna ru'd the sin yet,
            'That Friday's night.'

The widow then began to state
   All that had pass'd between them;
Whilk soon clear'd up the grand mistake,
   Shew'd Geordie where he'd been then.
He curst himsel' for sik a deed;
   And for lak o' discretion;
He wish'd some frosty cauld dike-head,
   Had been his habitation
            That Friday's night.

What cou'd he do? the day approach'd
    His widow turn'd a mammy;
And weel he kend it wad mair cost
    Than ony whalp or lammie.
He married her, and brought her hame,
    Upon a gude gray naggy;
But often Geordie rues the time,
    He cross'd the muir to Maggie
                    That Friday's night.

Now here's a health to 'onest Bess,
    And here's a health to Geordie;
And here's to ilka bony lass,
    That's constant to her wordie:
May peace and plenty be his lot,
    That loves his fellow-creature;
And warse than happen'd Geordie Scott,
    Meet ev'ry f——r,
                    On ony night.

SINGULAR DREAM,

from a correspondent

The other night, on my way home, after a fatiguing day, I stumbled into the house of an old acquaintance, on purpose to rest myself, as well as to find amusement in his conversation, until my usual time of going to bed. This friend of mine is a phenomenon of wisdom and foresight. He keeps a weekly, if not a daily register of all the undermining and unmannerly actions practised by the men and women of this metropolis and its environs, as far as his information serves him, and he spares no pains to gain that information; and consequently can, when he pleases, retail all the incidents that have led to the births, marriages, and deaths for twenty years bygone; as well as to all the failures in business, most of which he foresaw and prognosticated with the greatest punctuality. In a short time I was struck with astonishment at the man's amazing discernment, for though we were fellow collegians, and have long been known to one another, we have not been in habits of intimacy; and I did not use to hear him mentioned by associates with half so much deference as it appeared to me he was entitled to. I set him down in my mind as a most useful member of society, and from his extraordinary powers of estimating human characters, and human actions aright, one whom it would be wisdom for all men, both high and low, to consult before they formed any permanent connexion, or entered upon any undertaking of moment.

Impelled by a curiosity too natural, of seeing into futurity, I soon began to consult him about the affairs of the nation, and what was most likely to be the result of the present stagnation of trade, and measures of government. My heart thrills with horror to this hour, when I reflect upon the authentic and undeniable information which I received from him. We are all in the very jaws of destruction; our trade, our liberties, our religion, Heaven be our guard! our religion and all are hanging by one slender thread! which the flames of hell have already reached, and will soon singe in two. This was a shocking piece of intelligence for me, who had always cherished the fond idea that we were the most thriving and flourishing people on the face of the whole earth. When I was a young man, the several classes of society in this country were not half so well fed, clothed, or educated as they now are, what could I think but that we were a thriving and happy people? But instead of that, we were ruined bankrupts, prodigals, depraved reprobates, and the slaves of sin and Satan. Much need have the people of this land to be constantly upon their watch-towers, having their lamps trimmed, and their beacons burning; for indeed there is not one thing as it appears to be. Our liberty is a flam, our riches a supposition, and the Bank notes in fact not worth a halfpenny a piece. Improvements in the arts and sciences, or in rural and national economy, are no signs of prosperity, but quite the reverse. And, would you believe it? There are some gentlemen high in office, whom I, and most of the nation, have always regarded as men of the utmost probity—Lord help us, they are nothing better than confounded rascals! O! that we were wise, that we understood this!

Taught thus, by incontrovertible arguments, that the end of all things, at least with respect to Britain, was at hand, I gladly relinquished the disagreeable topic, and introduced the affairs of this city; yet I confess I did it with a good deal of diffidence, having learned to distrust my own powers of perception altogether, and consequently knew how unfit I was to judge of any thing from appearance. But how shall I ever describe to you the deformed picture, which was now for the first time placed before my astonished view! It is impossible; for it was one huge mass of inconsistence. I was plainly told, that our magistrates are no magistrates, but that they only suppose themselves so: that they are a set of gossipping, gormandizing puppies: that they are fast bringing the city to ruin, which must soon come to the hammer, and be sold to the highest bidder: that our ministers of the gospel are no ministers of the gospel — that they are drunkards, wine-bibbers, and friends of publicans and sinners — that there is not one sentence of pure gospel preached amongst them all! — and the holy sacraments are degenerated into a mere mock or matter of form; which those only condescend to accept, who, unable to preserve a character for any thing else, endeavour to scratch up one for devotion; what a miserable state our church must be in, thought I, when 'the *boar* that from the *forest* comes; doth waste it at his pleasure,'* I beg your pardon, Sir, I was not meaning you.

In the High Court of Session, too, where I supposed every thing to have been decided with equity and conscience, all is, it seems, conducted by intrigue, and

* *Psalms* 80.

the springs of justice directed by self-interest alone. But that which grieved me most of all was, what he told me of our ladies, those sweet, those amiable creatures, whom I had always fondly viewed as that link in the chain of creation which connected the angelic with the human nature. Alas, Sir! it seems that it is too true that Burns says; 'They're a' run w—s and jades thegither;' for my friend assured me, that they are all slaves to the worst of passions; and that they neither think nor act as if they were accountable creatures. He said that none of them ever employed a thought on any thing better, than by what means she might get a husband, or how most to plague one after she had him; and that when they were not ruminating on the one or the other of these, it was sure to be on something worse; and he cited an old foolish Roman in confirmation of his theory, who says, '*mulier quae sola cogitat, male cogitat.*'*

About this time another gentleman entered, who was without doubt come for the same purpose with myself, namely, to learn how mankind were behaving themselves on an average; and as he took up the conversation I remained silent, as indeed I had done for the most part of the time since I entered. My ideas being wound up to the highest pitch of rueful horror, I fell into a profound reverie, and from thence into a sound sleep, in which it seems I continued for nearly half an hour, and might have continued much longer, if they had not awakened me, on perceiving that I was labouring under the most painful sensations. The truth is, though I did not like to tell them all at that time, I

---

* 'A woman who thinks alone, thinks badly.'

had been engaged in a dreadful dream. There is an old Scotch proverb, that 'one had better dream of the deil than the minister;' but I dreamed of them both, and mixed them so completely together that they seemed to be one and the same person; but there is no accounting for these vagaries of fancy in the absence of reason.

I thought I was in a country church, where you have often been, Sir, and that I had just taken my seat in the pew where you and I have often sat and sung bass to the old tunes, which our old precentor lilted over to us; when, who should I see mount the pulpit to preach, but the very identical friend who sat discoursing beside me, and who had so lately opened my eyes to our ruined and undone state. He read out a text from the Scriptures with great boldness. I have forgot where he said it was, for indeed I thought he did not name the right book; but I remember some of the words, which run thus: 'Because our daughters are haughty, and walk with stretched forth necks, and wanton eyes, walking and mincing as they go, and making a *tripping* with their feet.' He read it twice over, and then I heard a tittering noise; when, looking over my shoulder, I saw the church filled with the most beautiful women I had ever beheld in my life! — I wept to think how bad miserable creatures they were all, that so much wickedness should be concealed under so sweet a veil, and that their parents should have been at so much pains bringing up so many pests to society, and objects fitted for destruction. But the more I looked at them, they became the more lovely, and the more I looked at the preacher, he became the more ugly, until I could no longer look at him without terror. At length a tall lady stretched forward her head, and whispered to me that he was the devil. I uttered a loud scream, and hid myself behind the pew, having a peculiar aversion to that august personage, and peeping through a hole, I beheld him change his form gradually from that of a human creature, into a huge black sow. He then stepped down from the pulpit, with some difficulty, and began feeding out of a deep trough. A thought struck me in a moment, that I might easily rid mankind of their greatest enemy, by felling him at one blow, before he observed me, for his head was quite out of sight: so, snatching down a grave-pole, I glided silently away to execute my cowardly purpose. When I came within stroke, I heaved my grave-pole, and collected my whole force for the blow. 'I'll do for you now, old boy,' said I to myself. At that very moment he lifted up his ugly phiz! and gave me such a look, that I was quite overcome with terror, and fled yelling along the area, and the devil after me. My knees grew extremely weak, and besides, I was so entangled among women and petticoats, that I sunk powerless to the earth, and Satan got hold of me by the arm. My friend, at that unlucky moment, observing my extraordinary agitation, took hold of my arm, and awaked me. My scattered senses not having got time to collect, I still conceived him to be the devil, and remembering the text, 'resist the devil, and he will fly from you,' I attacked my astonished friend with the most determined fury, boxing him unmercifully on the face, and uttering the most dreadful imprecations, resolved, it seems, that he should not insult me, or take me away with impunity. The other gentleman interfered, and brought me to my senses. 'What do you mean by such a rude and beastly attack, Sir?' said my friend, while the blood poured from his nose. 'I most humbly beg your pardon, Sir,' said I, 'but indeed I thought you was the devil.' 'Upon my word a very extraordinary excuse,' said he, 'I know I never had any great share of beauty to boast of, but I am not just so ugly as to be taken for the devil neither; and I am certainly entitled to expect an apology, both for your mad assault, and the whimsical excuse you have made for it.' He accompanied this sentence with a look so malicious, and, as I imagined, so like a fiend, that I was utterly disconcerted; and could only add, by way of palliation, that I believed I did not know what I was doing; so, bowing, I walked off rather abruptly, accompanied by the other gentleman, who was ready to burst with laughter, all the way down the stairs. — When we got to the street, 'Well,' said he, 'our friend certainly was to blame, but you have, without doubt, carried the jest rather too far. I believe, after all, that he has been speaking the truth of you, which has caused you to take it so ill.' 'Speaking the truth of me!' exclaimed I, 'what do you mean? I hope he was not assailing my character and foreboding my ruin while I was asleep?' 'Aye, that's very good,' said he, laughing; 'that's very good indeed; so you were indeed sleeping, and did not hear a word that he said?' 'Upon my honour, I did not hear a word that he said,' returned I. 'Oh! that is rather too bad, my dear Sir,' said he, continuing to laugh immoderately; 'why, what the devil was it then that offended you, and induced you to give him such a drubbing?' — 'The devil, I believe it was,' said I, and then began a long bungling story about my dream, at which he only laughed the more, being firmly established in the belief that the sleep was a sham, and the assault intentional, or at least that it was the consequence of my having been irritated past bearing, by his injurious reflections.

Now, as this business is soon to be made public, by being discussed in a court of justice, I intreat you to reserve a place in your Book of Tales for this letter, which I declare to you, upon my honour, contains the real and fair statement of the facts as they followed upon one another. I am cited to answer for entering the house of Mr A.T. philosopher, and teacher of the science of chance, without any previous invitation, interpellation, or intimation; but with an intention, as it would appear, of wounding, bruising, maiming, and taking away the life of the foresaid A.T. philosopher, and teacher of the science of chance; and for most feloniously, maliciously, and barbarously, threatening, cursing, and striking the said Mr A.T. philosopher, and teacher of the science of chance, to the effusion of his blood, the damage of his person and clothes, and the endangerment of his life; and that without any provocation on the part of the foresaid A.T. philosopher and foresaid of foresaids. Yet, notwithstanding of all this, and though my counsel assures me, that I will be found liable in expenses to a high amount, I hereby declare to you, and to the world, that I am conscious of no evil intention with regard to my friend the philosopher. I went with an intention of receiving amusement and instruction from his conversation. I believed all that he told me. — I fell asleep, — which was certainly a breach of good manners, but what demon put it into my head, that he was the devil I cannot tell; *certes*, I thought he was; and when a man acts from the best intentions, I do not think he is blame-worthy if the effect should sometimes prove different. It is very hard that a man should be severely fined for resisting the devil, when there are so few that give themselves the trouble to do it.

It is true, that owing to my country education, I am a little inclined to be superstitious; but I cannot help thinking, that the whole of the accident was a kind of judgment inflicted on us both for a dangerous error; on him for abusing so many of the human race behind their backs, who were in all probability better than he; and on me for assenting implicitly to all his injurious insinuations. Nay, I would even fain carry the mystery a little further, by alleging, that a traducer and backbiter is actually a limb or agent of the devil, and that the dream was a whisper conveyed to my fancy by one of those guardian spirits that watch over the affairs of mortal men. The strange combination of ideas which that foolish dream and its concomitant mischiefs have impressed on my mind, have, besides, given me a mortal aversion to the features and looks of my old acquaintance; it has likewise led me often to an examination of the apparent springs of this principle of detraction, and foreboding of evil from every action, whether public or private; and the more I think of it, the more firmly am I persuaded of its impropriety; and that whatever such foreseers may pretend, if their inferences point only towards evil, it is a symptom of a bad heart. 'Let no such men be trusted.'

We can form our opinions of that which we do not know, only by placing it in comparison with something that we do know: whoever therefore is over-run with suspicion, and detects, or pretends to detect artifice, in every proposal, must either have learned the wickedness of mankind by experience, or he must derive his judgment from the consciousness of his own disposition, and impute to others the same inclinations which he feels predominate in himself. Suspicion, however necessary, through ways beset on all sides by fraud and malice, has been always considered, when it exceeds the common measure, as a token of depravity. It is a temper so uneasy and restless, that it is very justly appointed the concomitant of guilt. It is an enemy to virtue and to happiness; for he that is already corrupt, will naturally be suspicious; and he that becomes suspicious will quickly be corrupt.

I was for the space of twenty years intimately acquainted with an old man named Adam Bryden, whose disposition and rule of behaviour, were widely different from those of the philosopher above mentioned, and I fear too many of the inhabitants of this metropolis. It was a maxim with him, which, though never avowed, was easily discovered, that if he could not say well of a person, he said nothing of them at all. Of the characters of the fair sex he was peculiarly tender in this respect, and always defended them against every probability. When the charges became too evident to be longer denied, he framed the kindest and most tender excuses for them, on account of the simplicity of their hearts, and kindness of their natures, which induced them to trust too implcitly to the generosity of others. It was impossible to be long in his company, without conceiving a higher opinion of the goodness of the Almighty, of his love and kindness towards his creatures, and of his wisdom displayed in the government of the universe. On the contrary, it is impossible to be long in the company of Mr A.T. the philosopher, without conceiving that Being who is all goodness, to be a tyrant, who has created man, and woman in particular, for the sole purpose of working mischief, and then of being punished eternally for that very mischievous disposition which is an ingredient in the composition of their natures. It was impossible to be long in company with the former without conceiving a higher opinion of the dignity of human nature, and of the happiness attainable by man, both in this life and that which is to come. It is impossible to be long in the company of the latter, without conceiving ourselves to be in a world of fiends, who have no enjoyment but in the gratification of sensual appetites, nor any hope but in the ruin of others.

Let your readers, then, Sir, consider seriously, which of these two characters appears to be most congenial to a heavenly mind; which of them is most likely to be productive of happiness and contentment in this life; and which of them is most conformable to the precepts left us by our great Lawgiver, in order to fit us for partaking of the blessings of a world to come. Let them weigh all these considerations impartially, and imitate the one or the other, as reason and revelation shall direct; but perhaps those who delight in magnifying the shades in the human character, may, in the end, be subjected to pay as dear, if not dearer, for it, than either Mr A.T. the philosopher, or your humble servant,

J.G.

LOVE ADVENTURES OF
MR GEORGE COCHRANE

*'Sans les femmes, les deux extremités de la vie
seraient sans secours, et le milieu sans
plaisirs.'* Rich*

It is well known to all my friends that I am an old
bachelor. I must now inform them further, that this
situation in life has fallen to me rather by accident than
from choice; for though the confession can hardly fail
to excite laughter, I frankly acknowledge, that there is
nothing I so much regret as the many favourable
opportunities which I have suffered to escape me of
entering into that state, which every natural and
uncontaminated bias of the human soul bears
testimony to, as the one our all-wise Creator has
ordained for the mutual happiness of his creatures.
Never does that day dawn in the east, shedding light
and gladness over the universe, nor that night wrap the
world in darkness and silence, on which I do not sigh
for the want of a kind and beloved bosom friend, whom
I might love, trust, and cherish, in every circumstance
and situation of life; to whom I might impart every
wish and weakness of my heart, and receive hers in
return; rejoice in her joy; share her griefs; and weep with
her over her own or the misfortunes of others, or the
general depravity of human nature; kneel with her at
the same footstool of infinite grace, and jointly implore

*"Without women, the two extremities of life would be without
succour, and the intervening years without pleasures.' Quotation
untraced.

forgiveness for our frailties and failings, and a blessing on our honest endeavours at fulfilling the duties of our station. But as the case now stands with me, I find myself to be an insignificant, selfish creature, unconnected to the world by any ties that can tend to endear it to me, further than the sordid love of life, or the enjoyment of some sensual gratification. I am placed, as it were alone, in the midst of my species; or rather like a cat in a large family of men, women, and children, to whose joys it bears witness, without being able to partake of them; and where no person cares a farthing for it, unless for his own benefit or amusement.

When lying on a bed of sickness, instead of experiencing the tender attention and indulgence which the parent or husband enjoys, I am left to languish alone, without one to bind up my aching head, or supply the cordial or cooling draught to my parched lips. Is not every old bachelor in the same situation? Yes, Horace says,

'Mutato nomine de te fabula narratur.'*

Whatever he may be made to believe, he certainly is. If he be a poor man, he is a burden upon his friends, an encumbrance which they would gladly be rid of by any means; if rich, his relations may smile and flatter him, but in their hearts they wish most devoutly for his death.

The married state, it is true, may be entered into with rashness and imprudence, especially in the heat and folly of youth; but in any way, it is more commendable than the selfish and unnatural principle

*'Change the name, and the story is about you' (from Horace's *Satires*, Book I, Satire I).

of shunning it altogether. In the worst case that can happen to a man, which is, when his selected partner turns out to be really disagreeable, still the family which she brings him engages his affection; his happiness becomes interwoven with theirs, and if he has been unfortunate in his connubial love, he enjoys the exhilarating sensations of parental affection with the more warmth and delicacy; so that still his family becomes a kind of stay whereon to rest for worldly enjoyments, and the star by which he is directed throughout the dangerous voyage of life.

The argument, that some are unhappy in this state, is of no avail; for there are many people in the world of such refractory and turbulent dispositions, that they will be unhappy in any state, and whose tempers will ever contribute, in a certain degree, to keep every one unhappy who is connected with them. Such people would probably be still more unhappy in any other state than that of wedlock, and such commonly are one, or both of the parties, who thus disagree. These are, however, only the worst cases that can happen; and though I myself am a bachelor, my opinion is fixed with respect to this. I am fully persuaded, that if there is any calm, unruffled felicity, within the grasp of an erring and imperfect creature, subject to so many passions, wants, and infirmities, it is to be found in the married state. That I have missed it, has certainly been my own blame; for I have been many times most desperately in love, and never yet met with an unfavourable reception.

The first time I fell in love was with a pretty girl who lived in our family, when I was scarce seventeen years of age. I never once thought of marrying her, nor even of informing her how much I loved: indeed I did not know myself what I wanted with her; but I could not stay out of her sight if it was possible for me to get into it. I always found some pretext of being where she was, though it had been only to pick a quarrel with her about some trifle. I could not endure to see any other man speak to her, or take the least notice of her whatever, and on every such occurrence wreaked my vengeance upon her.

The next time I fell in love was with one of the most lovely and amiable of the whole sex; but so far above my rank in life, that my cause appeared entirely hopeless. I however took every opportunity of being near to her, and was so overpowered with delight at seeing her, and hearing her speak, that the tears sometimes started to my eyes. I frequented the church every Sunday, and never once looked away from the front of the gallery where she sat. I commonly knew no more of what the parson was talking, than if he had been delivering himself in Greek. Nothing in nature gave me any delight that was not some way connected with her, and every thing that was so was dear to me; I heard with unspeakable delight, that, to the astonishment of the whole neighbourhood, she had positively rejected two gentlemen, each of whom had made her proposals of marriage highly advantageous.

I shall never, while recollection occupies her little tenement amongst the other powers of my mind, forget the day on which I first disclosed my passion to this dear and lovely woman! It was on the 20th of March. The day was sharp; and as I walked towards her father's mansion, I perceived her coming as if to meet me. I was wrapped in my tartan mantle, and was rather warm with walking, yet I was instantly seized with a fit of shivering. She, however, turned off at one side, and passed me at about the distance of twenty paces. She gave me only one look, but that was accompanied by a most bewitching smile, and went into a little summer-house. O how fain would I have followed her — but it was a piece of such monstrous rudeness to intrude upon a lady's privacy, that it quite startled me! — I thought upon the look which she gave me, and the bewitching smile! — Again I concluded that these were given only by chance — as she was always smiling. I spent about ten minutes in the utmost agony, resolving and re-resolving; and still she did not again make her appearance. At length, scarcely sensible, I likewise went into the little summer-house. She was sitting on one of the benches; her lovely cheek leaning on her hand; the train of her gown drawn over her shoulders; a book lay open before her; and the tears were standing in her eyes. I dare say I accosted her with a most sheepish look, saying, I was come in to see what detained her so long in that cold house on such a sharp day. She said, that she had by chance opened that book, which was so engaging that she could not quit it; and that it had cost her some tears. I stepped to the bench, going close up to her, merely to see what book it was — I had no other motive! It was *The Vicar of Wakefield*. It is a charming work, said I, and sat down *to read it along with her*. I could not see distinctly to read with the ends of the lines turned towards me; I never could read to any purpose that way; so I was obliged to sit excessively close to her, before I could attain the right point of view. We read on — not a single word passed betwixt us for several pages, save one, which was often repeated, it was, *Now*. She commonly ran over the pages faster

than I could, but always refrained from turning the leaf
until I cried — *Now*. I still could not see very well, and
crept a little closer to her side. I even found it necessary,
in order to *see* with *precision*, to bring my cheek almost
close to her's. What raptures of delight thrilled my
whole frame! — We read on — at least we looked over
the words, without taking any heed to them. This was
the case with me, and I believe with her, for she shed no
more tears. We came to the end of a chapter — '*Now*,'
said I; but it seems I had said it in a different way that
time, for, instead of turning the leaf, she closed the
book! This little adverb has many various meanings, all
of which are easily distinguished by the manner of
pronouncing it. 'I am weary of it,' said she. ' 'Tis time,'
said I. I envied not the joys of angels that day! when for
the first time I found myself alone with her whom I
loved and valued above all the rest of the world. I was so
electrified with delight, that for a moment I believed it
to be all a dream. I declared my violent affection for her,
in the most respectful manner I was capable of. She did
not receive the information with the smallest degree of
surprise, but as something she was previously well
acquainted with. I mentioned that her distinguished
and admired personal excellencies, together with her
elevated rank in life, had hitherto restrained me from
making known my love to her; as it also entirely
precluded the least chance of my ever attaining her as
my wife. Think how I was astonished at receiving the
following answer: — 'The sea, to be sure, is very deep,
but he is a great coward who dares not wade to the knee
in it!' — 'What do you say, madam?' said I. — She
repeated the sentence. 'But do you say this in earnest?'
said I. 'Indeed I do,' said she, firmly, while her eyes were

fixed on the ground. I clasped her to my bosom, and I do not know what extravagant nonsense I uttered amid the excess of joy with which I was transported.

During the space of three years we were seldom asunder, and enjoyed all the delights of the most pure and tender affection. I placed implicit confidence in her; and she received me always with the most enchanting kindness and good humour; and even, when she once learned that I had been paying my addresses to another, she did not in the least resent it, but observed, that it was no more than she expected; for that she knew me better than I knew myself. I had long been pressing her most ardently to name a day for our marriage, and at length she condescended to refer it entirely to me. Will any person, even the most dead to every sense of honour, gratitude, or love, believe that I could ever abandon this angel of a woman? — To my everlasting shame and confusion, I acknowledge that I did; and it is a just award of Providence, that I now sigh for that mutual interchange of hearts, which I can no more enjoy. I first fixed on one day for our nuptials — then another — and another. I knew I was sure of her whenever I pleased, and grew more and more careless. Her behaviour to me continued the same, without the smallest abatement of cheerful condescension: never did a single murmur, or a bitter remonstrance escape from her lips, nor one frown of dissatisfaction cloud her brow: and when, at last, my total neglect threw her into the arms of another, who was more deserving of her, still her behaviour remained unchanged; and to this day she receives me as an old friend whom she is glad to see. May Heaven smile on that benign face, which never wore a frown but in contempt of vice or folly; and bestow upon her kind and tender heart that peace and happiness which she so well merits, and to which mine must now ever continue a stranger. I feel my loss the more keenly, by knowing it was once in my power to have enjoyed that happiness which I threw away.

I have, since that period, been several times very deeply in love; sometimes for a fortnight, sometimes for a month, but never exceeding the space of half a year. Some of my adventures with the fair sex have been so whimsical, that I do not think I can divert my readers better, than by relating as many of them as this paper will contain.

I at one time conceived a violent affection for a lady whom I chanced to accompany from Edinburgh in the stage-coach. The marked attention which I paid to her at the stages and by the way, gained so much upon her heart, that she granted me permission to visit her, providing I kept out of her father's sight. This is not an example which I can recommend to my fair readers for their imitation; for indeed, I think, if any of them are admitting of the visits of a lover, of whom they would be ashamed to a father or brother, they would do as well not to admit them at all. But so it was in this instance, and she could not have annexed a condition that pleased me better, as he was a haughty, proud man, and no very warm friend of mine. After many contrivances, we both agreed that the night season was the best and most convenient for us to meet. Perhaps my Edinburgh readers will be startled at this agreement; but it is a fact, that every young woman in the country must be courted by night, or else they will not be courted at all; whatever is said to them on that subject during the day, makes no more impression upon them than stocks or stones, but goes all for nothing, or mere words of course. I was so impatient for this interview, that I got very little rest until I set about it. So one dark winter night, I wrapped myself in my father's chequered plaid, mounted his bay mare, and away I rode to see this new mistress of my heart. I fastened my father's bay mare in a dell, at a distance from the house, which I approached cautiously on foot about eleven at night. As chance directed, the front door was standing open, and as I was necessitated to take some bold step, I slipped off my shoes, took them in my hand, and stole quietly up stairs into her room, where I determined to wait her arrival. It was, however, a place where, in case of a wrong individual entering, there was not the slightest screen where I could take shelter. I was not altogether at my ease — the people bustled about from one room to another — opened doors, and closed them again, each time with a most terrible noise — every one of them went to my heart like a cannon-shot. In my heart, I wished the people all in the deepest and darkest hollow of — their beds. My terrors increased — I durst not sit longer — so again taking my wet shoes in my hand, and my father's chequered plaid below my arm, I slipped quietly up to a garret-room filled with household articles. I was perfectly safe there, and quite at my ease, as no person slept in it; so, laying my wet shoes on the lid of a large chest, and wrapping my father's chequered plaid around my shoulders, I sat down on an old settee, laden with men's clothes on the back. I had not tarried there above three minutes, until I heard a foot coming lightly up the stair, while the approaching light let me see how thick the rafters stood which supported the roof. I was sure it was the foot of my charming maiden, for it sounded scarcely so loud as a rat's in the ceiling. I flew with joy to meet her, or to enter the room at or near the same time with herself. — O! misery, death, and destruction! Who was it? — No other than the very person, among all the sons of men, whom I dreaded! Yes, it was the young lady's father, coming straight to my garret-room without his hat and shoes, and having a large candle burning in his hand. It was all over with me — to make my escape from the garret-room was impossible; but not having one moment to lose, as a last resource, I jumped in behind the old settee, and coured down as close as I possibly could. I saw him approaching, and marked the most deadly symptoms of revenge in every feature. He took up my wet shoes, turned them round and round in his hand with some marks of astonishment. Now, thought I to myself, what shall I do? or what shall I say? Shall I say I came to rob the house? or steal into his lovely daughter's chamber in the dark? — Any of them is bad enough — so die I must without an alternative! — He turned about — came to the old settee, where I had taken refuge — held over the candle! — O Lord! extend thy — I won't write another word on the subject — I really meant, when I began, to finish this story; but, I think, I must in all conscience be sunk low enough in the esteem of my readers already; and, will it not do as well to leave the conclusion of the prayer, and the conclusion of the adventure likewise, to the imagination? and then every one will paint the conclusion as best suits his own disposition. It is visible, from my writing of this, that I escaped: so the charitable will suppose me to have escaped unhurt, determining never to engage in the like again; the licentious will suppose me violating every principle of morality, as well as the innate postulate of honour and truth planted in the human breast by the Almighty, as a guard over open, kind, and unsuspecting innocence; and taking an undue advantage over a warm and feeling heart, to make that heart for ever miserable. The malicious will suppose me dragged down stairs — horse-whipped — ducked in the water — and set at liberty. Upon the whole, I find the truth will scarcely be worse than six out of seven among all the constructions that will be put upon it, therefore, on second thoughts, it will be better to go on. The truth then is, (for the whole story is absolute truth) that he held over the candle, and his head too; but it so happened, that either the clothes, or rather I think the beams of the candle, hindered him from seeing me. This was the greatest miracle I ever witnessed, for I was sitting perfectly open, staring him in the face like a hare, and watching, with terror, every motion of his eye. He turned the clothes over and over — selected a coat and over-alls from the heap — went down stairs whistling *Johnny Cope*, and gave me the greatest relief I ever experienced.

The lady came up shortly after — I attended her — was upbraided for my temerity — spent a short space with her in the most harmless and uninteresting chat, mostly about my getting out of the house, which was as absolutely necessary, as it was notoriously dangerous. 'It is next to impossible,' said she, 'for, as you have three bolted doors to open, the dogs will, at the first, be all about you; and if they do not worry you outright, will certainly awaken my father, who will have you by the neck in a moment.' 'I wish women never had been made,' said I; 'or that they had not been made so extremely beautiful, for I see they will be my ruin. But,

if I were once out' ——— She did not let me finish the
sentence: 'I'll let you out at once,' said she; 'you always
make so much ado about nothing.' Then pushing her
window gently up, which was straight above the front
door, she took hold of my father's chequered plaid, and
desired me to let myself down by it, while she would
hold by one end until I reached the ground. She
wrapped my wet shoes in the end of the plaid next her,
to enable her to keep her hold, and set her knee to the
wall to be ready. I crawled out, with my feet foremost,
requesting her by all means to keep a good hold. 'What
are you afraid of?' said she; 'I'll hold it if you were
double the weight that you are.' The window had no
weights, being kept up by a catch on one side; and as it
had been put gently up, the catch had only got a slight
hold. What it was that agitated it, I do not know; but at
the very moment on which I slid from the window, and
had begun to lay my weight to the plaid, down came the
window with a crack like a pistol! Whether it struck my
charmer's fingers, or only startled her, was a matter of
small importance to me, for I was doomed to abide by
the bitter consequences either way. In short, the
window and I came down precisely at the same time.
The thing that I next felt, was the stone stair at the
front door, on which my loin and shoulder struck with
a dead thump; and at the same instant one of my shoes,
which were none of the lightest, hit me on the face, and
the other on the breast; for the plaid, having come off
with a sudden jerk, brought them down with redoubled
velocity. From the stone stair of the front door I
tumbled heels-over-head down to the gravel, and took
it for granted that I was dead. I was not long, however,
in getting to my knees, in which position I remained a

long time, considering whether I was killed or not. The dogs barked within the house as if a whole kennel had broken loose. The goodman threatened them loudly, and ordered silence. — The doors now began to open within. — I was fain to get up, bruised as I was, and indeed I was wofully bruised, and taking my wet shoes in my hand, and my father's chequered plaid below my arm, and perceiving, to my astonishment, that all my bones were whole, I never once looked over my shoulder until I reached my father's bay mare. She was standing, capering and cocking her ears, in the dell, where she left a good many indelible marks of her impatience.

The next time I met with the young lady was in a large company, where there was a number of her own sex. After saluting them round, I turned to her — 'You little mischief,' said I, 'what made you let go?' The mentioning of this abruptly in the midst of company, and the ludicrous scene recurring to her imagination, had the effect of throwing her into a convulsion of laughter, out of which she could not recover till obliged to retire. An explanation was asked, but that was impossible to give; and many of the party, I believe, formed conjectures of their own, which, I am sure, were all wide of the truth.

I still continued very bad in love with her; and, as I had reason, from farther experience, to be more and more terrified for her father; therefore I had nothing for it but to use some shifts to see her privately. These were not easily obtained. However, she was fond of variety, and not greatly averse to my schemes. I got a few minutes conversation with her one day, and begged her to name a time when I could call and have a private uninterrupted chat with her. She told me the thing was impossible, and she would consent to no such thing. Besides, there was not a night in the year on which her father staid from home all night, save on *the eve of Lockerbie fair*, when he was obliged to stay from home all night to sell his lambs; but she would not for the world that I should come that night, as there was not a man about *the town* (so we always denominate a farm-steading.) Delighted with this sly prohibition, I shook her hand, and bade her good bye.

O how I longed for the eve of Lockerbie fair! Does any body know what the eve of a fair day, or any other day, means? I wish the reader to settle this in his own mind before he proceeds a sentence farther, and to settle it impartially; for it is a matter that may concern him deeply to understand, and it concerns me particularly that he should understand it.

I did not take my father's bay mare with me that day, but went along the heights, carrying my gun like a fowler, but without any dog. I did not shoot any muirfowl, nor did I wish to shoot any: When I am in love, all kind of noise and disturbance are distressing to me. I love silence and solitude — to be in languor, and think and dream of her that I admire — of all her beauties, sweets, and perfections. Imagination does very much for the women in this way; for I have myself transformed a girl, very little above ordinary, into a being of the most angelic loveliness; and have talked of her with such raptures to others, that they were obliged to view her in the same light; as no one ever disputed my good taste in female beauty. But this girl to whom I was so much attached, excelled every thing. O, she was so clever — so full of animation — had such eyes, such a shape, such a smile! — Good Lord! I wondered how any man, with common feelings of humanity, could live without her! For my part, I found that I could not, and I was determined that I would not live without her, let them all do as they would.

I came at length to the hill opposite to her father's house, where I lay in a bush, and watched the doors and windows with as much anxiety as a devout heathen ever did rising of the sun. If she would only but take a walk up the side of the river, thought I, I would slide down the back of the hill and meet with her; or if she walked down the river, I would follow her. But, above all, were she to take a walk up the glen, by the side of the planting. O, ye powers of love! to lead the lovely creature into that planting, far from the eyes of all living, and from her surly father's in particular — Then, to see her frown, and hear her chide, and protest that she would not go into the planting with any man on earth, far less with me, and all the while walking faster forward into the thicket than I could keep up with her. What delightful probabilities a lover fancies! She neither walked up the river that I might meet with her, nor down the river that I might follow her, nor up the glen that I might woo her in the planting; for she did not even come out of the house that I could see the whole afternoon. I saw several other females sauntering about in a careless indifferent manner, but they were coarse vulgar creatures, cast in moulds so different from that of my charmer, that they appeared rather like beings of another species. I had no patience with them; and was obliged several times to hide my face among the bent and the heather, that I might not see their round waists, and thick bare ancles as red as carrots, and thereby mar my ideas of the beauty and purity of the sex. I made several love verses while lying on the hill that evening, which I thought very good. One of them, which I made on seeing these vulgar menials going waddling about, run thus:

'I have looked long, I have looked sore
For the girl that I do adore;
But my beloved I cannot see —
I have found but the draff where the corn should be.'

Another, and perhaps a more original verse, ran thus:

'Oh! an my love were that heather bell
    That blooms upon the cowe,
Then I would take her in my arms
    Like a new clippit yowe;

And whatsoever we did do,
    To no man I would tell;
But I would kiss her rosy lips,
    As I do that heather bell.'

The great art in making poetry, you will observe, is to *round the verse well off*. If the hindmost line sounds well, the verse is safe. I have never known any man who was so much master of that particular knack as myself, of which I could give many instances as well as the above, if I had leisure from more important matters.

It happened to be a particularly long afternoon that on which I lay watching for my charmer. The sun stood still about the same place for several hours, whether on account of any imperative command, or sheer ill-will, I do not know; but it is absurd to suppose that his course is regulated by any stated time. I have seen a very material difference in the celerity of his journeying. If any disbelieve me, let him ask a school boy, whether the afternoon of Friday or Saturday is the longest? Ask the maid-servant, whether the fair day, or the day that she is toiling on the harvest field, wears first or fastest to a close? but, above all, ask the lover who is sitting watching for the fall of night, that he may meet and clasp her whom he admires above all the rest of the world.

After much procrastination, the sun at last went down, and the twilight followed with slow and lingering pace. With a beating heart I again approached the house. 'There will be none of these boisterous dogs here to-night,' thought I; 'the shepherds will be all absent at Lockerbie fair.' The thought was barely formed ere I was attacked by two in a most vociferous manner, as I stood by the garden-wall cowering like a bogle. I tried to cajole them in a whisper, pretending to be friends with them. It would not do, they waxed louder and louder. I threw stones at them — they were worse than ever — 'Bow — wow — wow. Yough, yough.' I was obliged to take to my heels and fly, for the inmates were getting alarmed. The women rushed out; I heard their voices, but could not see them distinctly — my dear angel was among them. 'Who can that be?' I heard one saying. 'Only some passenger going home from the fair,' returned she in a voice sweeter than music. 'I hope he means to ca' in,' said the other, in a loud giggling, vulgar voice; 'he'll surely gie some o' us a bode as he gaes by.' 'Na, na,' cried another gawky, 'he hasna sae muckle in him; he's awa wi' his tail atween his legs like Macmillan's messan.' My dear angel then called in the dogs, and rebuked them both by name as they passed her; and after desiring her women to keep their jokes within the walls of the house, as they knew not who might hear them, she went in last, and closed the door. Every word that she spoke thrilled my heart with delight; and I was utterly impatient for the hour of meeting — no jealous father to alarm us — no rival to interpose; not even a man-servant about the house; and as for the maids, they had a fellow-feeling for each other; and moreover, she had it in her power to make them do what she pleased.

Urged by this hopeful consideration, I was not long in returning to her window, at which I tapped lightly, my very breath almost clean gone with anxiety. She threw up the sash. I accosted her in a tremulous broken whisper — 'My dear, dear Mary,' said I, 'have I found you alone?' 'Bless me, Mr Cochrane,' said she aloud, 'is it you? Why do you rap at the window rather than the door? Come in, come in; my father, I dare say, will be very glad to see you.' I was stupified and speechless. 'There is some vile mistake here,' thought I. But before I recovered the dear teazing creature opened the door, and bidding me come in, I implicitly obeyed and followed her into the parlour. — 'Where have you been, or where are you going so late?' said she. 'What need have you to ask,' said I, 'Mary? You know well enough that I am come to bear you company for a little while. Did not you tell me that your father and all the men were to be from home to-night?' 'Me!' exclaimed she, 'I never told you such a thing! I could not tell you that, for I knew it was impossible. I was afraid you would come last night; for, it being the fair eve, there was not a man about the town — the two maids were away on some business of their own, and here was I for the whole night locked up in the house, without a living soul in it but myself. Positively I do not know what I should have done, if you had come last night.'

I am certain there was never another wooer looked so sheepish as I did at this moment. I was chagrined past endurance at myself, at her, and at all mankind. I saw the golden opportunity was past, and that I had run my head into a noose, and consequently I was in a violent querulous humour. She was no less so. 'My dear Mary,' said I, 'surely you will not pretend to assert that the evening of a fair day is not the fair eve!' 'Are you so childishly ignorant,' returned she, 'as not to know that the eve of a festival, holiday, or any particular day whatever, always precedes the day nominally?' I denied the position positively, in all its parts and bearings. She reddened; and added, that she could not help pitying a gentleman who knew so little of the world, and the terms in use among his countrymen — terms with which the meanest hind in the dale was perfectly well acquainted. 'Pray, consider,' added she, 'do you not know that the night before a wedding, the night on which we throw the stocking, is always denominated the wedding eve? All-Hallow eve, the night on which we burn the nuts, pull the kail stocks, and use all our cantrips, is the evening before Hallow-day. St Valentine's eve, and Fasten's eve, are the same. Why then will you set up your own recent system against the sense and understanding of a whole country?'

'Never tell me of your old Popish saws and customs; the whole of your position is founded in absurdity, my love,' said I. 'This, you know, is the evening of the fair day — the fair is doubtless going on as merrily as ever; this then must either be the fair eve, or else the fair has two eves, which is rather more than either common sense or use and wont will warrant.'

I found I had acted very wrong; for by this time anger was depicted on her lovely countenance, and I saw plainly that she had a smithy spark of temper in her constitution.

'I could go farther back, and to higher authority, than old Popish saws, as you call them, for the establishment of my position, if I chose,' said she; 'I could take the account of the first formation of the day and the night, where you will find it recorded, that "the *evening* and the morning were the first day;" but as it would be a pity to mortify one by a confutation who is so wise in his own conceit, I therefore give up the argument. You are certainly in the right; and may you always profit in the same way as you have done now, by sticking to your own opinion.'

This was a severe one; and in the temper and disposition that I was in, not to be brooked. 'Nothing can be more plain,' said I, 'than that the evening of a day is the evening of that day.'

'Nothing can,' said she.

'And, moreover,' said I, 'has not the matter been argued thoroughly by our christian divines?'

'It has,' said she.

'And have not they all now agreed, from St Chrysostom down to Ebenezer Erskine, that the Sabbath-day begins in the morning?'

'They have,' said she.

'And if the Sabbath begins in the morning, so must also Monday; and so must every day, whether fair day or festival.'

'There is no doubt of it at all,' said she; 'wherefore

reason any more about the matter? Here is my father coming, we shall appeal to him, and he will, without doubt, ratify all that you have been saying.' Her father now entered; for he had been all the while in the next room settling his fair accounts. His eyes were heavy with fatigue, and his face red with sunburning and whisky punch — a most ungainly figure he was. 'Humph!' said he, as he came in, 'wha hae we gotten here?' 'It is Mr Cochrane, sir, who stepped in on his way home from the moors to get the news of the fair; but what argument think you he has taken up? he will not let me say that this is the fair eve.' 'Neither it is, Miss,' said he, 'any body knows that the night afore the fair is the fair e'en.' 'I can hardly trow that you are right, sir,' said she. 'Nor can I, upon my honour,' said I. 'Ye canna, upon your honour, can ye no? Humph! sic honour! Fine honour, faith! Crocks wad craw an duds wad let them. Ye're unco late asteer, I think, the night, chap. — Whar hae ye been scatterin focks sheep the day?' I assured him that I had molested no one's sheep, for that my dog had left me, and that I had had very little sport.

'Sport! snuff's o' tobacco!' exclaimed he, 'to hear some folk tauk o' sport that it wad suit better to be weeding their minnie's kail-yard, or clouting their ain shoon.'

'Humph! fine sport, faith! Ye surely hae unco little to do at hame.' I could hardly sit all this, but unwilling to break, both with the old gentleman and her I loved so passionately at once, I restrained myself, and answered him in a forced jocular manner. We got some supper; and the young lady proposed that we should drink a jug of toddy together afterwards, but this he positively declined, saying that I would be too late before I got home. This was as broad a hint for me to go about my business as could be given, and I would have been obliged to have taken it, had not sheer good manners compelled the young lady to propose that I should take a bed till the morning. Thinking this offer augured well, and that I would still be favoured with a private conference, I accepted of the proposal; but, without the possibility of getting another private word of her, I was shewn to my bed.

It was on the same floor with that of my charmer; her father's, as is before mentioned, being on the ground floor. I thought it behoved me, after coming so far to see her, to make an attempt at a private interview, and had no doubt but that she intended it, when she urged me to stay, notwithstanding the ill humour we both were in about the fair eve. I only threw off my coat and shoes, and laid me down on my bed; but to think of sleeping, so situated, was out of the question.

I lay till near midnight, when all was quiet, and not so much as a mouse stirring; then rose, put on my coat, and groped my way with great caution to her room, weening that she would have lain down without undressing like myself; but I was mistaken. I waked her — she pretended great astonishment and high displeasure, but always spoke below her breath. She said I was mad — and that it was fine behaviour in sooth — and a great number of such kind of things. I said still a greater number of the most extravagant things that ever were spoke, to all of which she only replied, 'go away to your bed, I tell you.' 'My dear divine Mary,' said I, 'as you know you are safe from insult in my company at all times, and in all situations, therefore why not suffer me to remain a while with you.'

'Because my father is jealous of us, and your peril, as well as mine, is very great. I must first remove that jealousy, and then you may come as often as you will,' she replied.

'O, for Heaven's sake, do remove that jealousy! I'll come every night to see you,' said I.

'You must then abide by the consequences,' she returned.

'I will abide by any consequences, for the sake of enjoying your sweet company without interruption,' said I.

'Well then,' she returned, 'I intreat that, in the first place, you will behave as you ought to do, and go to your bed. You *shall* go to your bed, I insist on it — you might have come on the fair eve, as a true lover and a man of sense would have done.'

'So I have, my dear, I have come on the fair eve;' said I.

I fear this was a unfortunate speech of mine, for, short as it was, it led to very disagreeable consequences. I declare that I had no more intention of going into the bed beside the young lady, than I had of again letting myself out at her window. I wanted only to have a private conference, for I loved her to distraction, and the most that I would have ventured would have been to have put my arm round her waist, and perhaps kissed her hand or her cheek. But at this luckless time, my arm happened to be flung over her shoulder above the clothes; at which, being offended, she flung back away from me. Thinking this was all a pretence, and that she wanted to make room for me — what could I do? I certainly did make a lodgement on the foreside of the bed. I was confoundedly mistaken, for at that moment my ears were saluted by a distant tinkling sound; but I thought they themselves were ringing, my spirits being in such commotion, and I paid no attention to the portentous sound. My charmer fled farther away from me, and I followed proportionally, still keeping, however, a due distance. The ill-set creature had a bell-handle at the back of her bed, which I little dreamed of, and far less that she would make any use of such a thing if she had. I had never found it the nature of the fair sex to be ready in exposing the imprudencies of their lovers, if committed for the sake of their own persons; therefore my astonishment may be judged of, when I heard a distant bell ringing fiercely and furiously. 'Good God!' said I, 'what's that?' She had not time to answer me, when her father entered, half dressed, and apparently only half awake, carrying a lighted candle, before which he held his open hand lest it should go out, and at the same time stared over above it, with open mouth, and his night-cap raised on his brow. 'Mary, my dear, what is the matter? what do you want?' said he. 'I want you, sir, to show this gentleman back to his bed-room,' said she. 'He has come here by some mistake, and refuses to go away. He even insists on lying in the same bed with me, a freedom which I *will not* admit of.' 'Fine behaviour, faith!' said the old savage, but not in particularly bad humour. He seemed pleased with his daughter's intrepidity, whom hitherto I suppose he had trusted but very little in love matters; and not less pleased to find me exposing myself in such a base manner, for which I could have no excuse. 'Humph!' continued he, 'you did very right, daughter.

Fine honour, faith! come awa chap, an' I'll shew you a gate that will set ye better. Humph! my certy! ye're ane indeed.' 'I hope, my dear sir,' said I, 'you cannot suspect me of any dishonourable intentions towards your daughter, whom, I declare, I love better than my own life!' 'Humph! fine love, faith! Come awa; sic love canna stand words.' So saying, the old hound seized me by the collar behind, and began to drag me away. 'What do you mean sir?' said I; 'I'll not be handled in this manner — I'll fight you, sir.' 'O, to be sure you will,' returned he. 'So will I — I'll fight too; but we maun do ae thing afore another, ye ken.' And then, with a ruder grasp, he dragged me down the stair, quite choaked by the gripe he had of my collar, and scarcely able to move my limbs. 'It is your own house, sir,' said I, 'else I would beat you most unmercifully — I would beat you like a dog.' 'Oh, to be sure, you would,' said he; 'there's nae doubt o't ava.' He then pushed me out at the door, giving me a furious kick behind; and then closing the door with a loud clash, he bolted it on the inside.

I was perfectly deranged, at having thus made a fool of myself; and, like all men who make a fool of themselves, I made a still greater fool of myself. I turned in a horrid rage, and ran to his window. 'Give me out my clothes, you old dog,' I cried. 'Give me out my shoes, my hat, my plaid, and my gun, or I'll break every window and door in your house, you old ragamuffin scoundrel that you are!' Clink went one pane of the window — jingle went another — I then heard a step inside, and, on pricking up my ears, I heard these words, 'By G—— I will give it him.' This brought me a little to my senses. I stood aside for a few seconds, and listening, I heard a window of the second flat opened softly, and soon beheld, between me and the sky, the muzzle of a gun coming sliding out. It was needless to bid me take to my heels; so I turned the corner and ran with main speed. The noise I made had wakened the shepherds who slept in the stable, and just as I ran past the door, out sallied two men and four dogs on me. 'Seize that rascal, and duck him,' cried their master, setting his head out at the window, 'he has broken up the house.' The two fellows ran after me; but I redoubled my speed; and being ready stripped for the race, I left them a considerable space behind. For some time the chase continued down a level valley, on which I had the heels of them, as the saying is, considerably; but, on leaving that, we came to rough boggy ground interspersed with some sheep-drains. I then heard the panting and blowing of one of the shepherds, who had gained ground, and was coming hard on me. The other was quite behind; and was laughing so immoderately that he could make little speed. I cast a hurried glance behind me, and saw a large brawny rascal within a dozen yards of me, who was bare-headed and bare-legged, and had a huge two-handed staff heaved above his right shoulder. I strained every nerve; and coming to a steep place, I went down it with inconceivable velocity. My pursuer did the same; but either his body came faster down than his feet could keep up with, or, what is as probable, he had set his foot inadvertently, in the height of his speed, into a drain, for down he came with such force, that he actually flew a long way in the air like a meteor before he alighted, and then pitched exactly on his nose and forehead. With such an unwonted force did he fly forward, after losing his equilibrium, that the staff, which he carried above his shoulder, came by me

with a swithering noise like that made by a black-cock
on the wing at full flight. I suppose he quitted it in his
swing, in order to save his face by falling on his hands.
Hard as my circumstances were, I could not help
laughing at my pursuer's headlong accident; but I lifted
the cudgel, and fled as fast as I could. Whether he was
hurt or only had his wind cut by his fall, I know not, but
I saw no more of him. About a mile farther on I heard
their voices behind me, but they were not so near as to
alarm me, and besides, I was in possession of the club,
which I had resolved to make use of, if attacked.

When out of danger, I deliberated calmly on what
had passed. I deemed myself very ill used — most
shabbily used! and my first emotions were toward a
stern and ample revenge. But when I began to question
myself about my motives, and answer these questions
strictly according to the dictates of honour and
conscience, I found that the answers did not entirely
satisfy me; and I was not so sure whether I had received
any thing beyond my deserts or not. 'What were you
going to do with the girl, George? Did you mean
honourably by her?' 'Oh, strictly.' 'That is, you
positively intended to make her your wife?' 'No.' I
searched every crevice of my heart out and in, and could
not say that I did. But then, I could not be happy out of
her company — in short, I loved her. Was not that
quite sufficient? Will said it was — honour said not
much about it; but conscience whispered the old
father's saying into my heart, 'Fine love, faith!'

'Suppose you had a lovely and beloved daughter,
George, and found a young fellow, of whose principles
and honour you did not much approve, who had stolen
clandestinely into her bed-chamber, and, in spite of

remonstrance, was even making his way into her bed, what would you have done with him? Aye, there's the rub! That brings the matter home at once! Cut his throat to be sure; besides stabbing him in different parts of the body. Fine love, faith!'

The thing that chagrined me most of all, was an indistinct recollection, that while the father was dragging me out of the room like a puppy by the neck, and I was threatening to fight him, I heard my sweetheart tittering and laughing. This almost drove me mad — it looked so like a set plan to make a fool of me. Yet I could not believe but that I had received some proofs of her attachment — proofs that I had preference in her esteem, or she must be a very extraordinary girl. 'Perhaps,' thought I again, 'all this shame and obloquy has sprung from the contradiction I gave her about *Lockerbie fair eve*. But, say that this is the case, it argues very little for her prudence or good sense.' Upon the whole, I found my admiration of her mixed with a little bitterness, and I formed some resolutions concerning her, not the most generous, nor the most commendable in the world.

Next morning I appeared at breakfast with a sullen, dissatisfied look. 'Sauf us! Geordie, what ails ye the day?' said my mother, 'ye look at a' things as ye coudna help it. An' guid forgie us! what hae ye made o' your hat, that ye are gaun wi' that auld slouch about your lugs? an' hae ye tint your shoon, that ye maun be strodgin about i' your boots?' I did not know how to satisfy my mother's curiosity, far less how to recover my apparel, without exposing myself and all concerned to both families; so, in the first place, I was obliged to contrive a manifest lie to pacify my mother. I told her, that while I was out on the moors, on such and such a height, by came William Tweedie's hounds hard after a fox; and that, in order to keep up with them, I had thrown away my plaid, shoes, hat, coat, and gun, and followed them all the way to Craigmeken Skerrs, where the hounds lost the foot; but on returning, it was that dark, that I found it impossible to get my clothes and gun; I had, however, left word with some of the shepherds, who I trusted would find them.

That same day there was a small packing-box left at the shop near by, directed to a man in Moffat, with a card for me. It was in these terms: 'M.I.'s Comp_{ts} to Mr C., sends the clothes in box. Will hide the gun till owner calls. No one shall know. Is sorry the consequences turned out so severe. Jealousy now asleep for ever. Mr C. needs not be in a hurry in taking advantage of this. When he does, let him throw a handful or two of gravel against a certain window.'

'Woman's an inexplicable thing!' said I to myself; 'Is it possible that the minx has exposed me to this shame and indignity, merely to lull alseep all jealousy in her father's breast with respect to me, that we may in future enjoy one another's company without fear or interruption. The thing is beyond my comprehension! She certainly is an extraordinary, and rather a dangerous girl this! However, I'll go and see her once more, and if I have such opportunities as I have had, I shall make better use of them.'

I was much pleased with her ingenuity in sending me my clothes; but the more I studied her, the less I could make of her character; yet she was a charming girl, nevertheless! It was not long till I again mounted my father's bay mare at night, and rode away to see her;

and, as she had given me the hint, when all was quiet I went and threw two handfuls of sand against her bed-room window. It was not long before she looked out, and, on seeing who it was, she made a sign with her hand to the door. I threw off my shoes and hid them, and then went to the door, where soon the dear delightful creature came, and opened it so softly, that I did not hear it, though standing at the landing-place, or *door-step*, as they call it there. Without speaking a word, she took me by the hand, pulled me in, and closed the door, but did not bolt it for fear of noise; then leading me up the stair, she ushered me darkling into her room, into that room where I had suffered so severely twice before, and which I did not enter again without trepidation and some uneasy apprehensions. She was elegantly dressed in a white night-gown, with a handsome house cap on her head, garnished with ribbons. I held her by the hand, and as I looked in her face, by the help of the moon that shone on her casement, I thought her the handsomest creature on earth. I sat down on a chair, and took her on my knee, clasping my arms around her waist. She made no resistance to this arrangement of position, amorous as it was; and to make it still worse, she leaned her head on my shoulder. I said many extravagantly fond things, to which she made no reply. Her behaviour always led me into errors. I deemed that the position in which we were placed, warranted me in snatching a kiss from those sweet delicious lips that were actually shedding the fragrance of roses and honey-suckle warm on my cheek; so I made the attempt. No — no such liberties could be granted; 'I disapprove of kissing altogether,' said she; 'and cannot tell you how much I admire the substitute resorted to by a certain valued friend of mine. Have not you heard of one, who, in cases of necessity, kissed a heather cowe?' I declared I never had: On which she repeated these two lines, with a softness and pathos that made them more ridiculous than aught I had ever heard:

'Then I would kiss her rosy lips,
As I do that heather bell!!!'

'Where the devil did you come by that?' said I. 'No matter how I got it,' replied she; 'I get many things that you are not aware of.' 'I believe you never said a truer thing in your life,' said I; 'I always thought you were a witch. But surely you will grant me a kiss of that comely cheek, which is a small boon; after I have come so often and so far to see you, you cannot refuse me when I ask so little?' 'O yes!' said she, with a deep feigned sigh,

'Man wants but little here below
Nor wants that little long.'

'The devil is in this girl!' thought I to myself; 'she is quite beyond my depth. I know not what to make of her!' I sat silent for some time, considering what she could mean. At that instant I thought I heard a kind of distant noise in the house, and at the same time, I observed that she was holding in her breath in the act of listening. I was going to ask her what it was; but she prevented me by laying her hand on my mouth, and crying 'hush!' I then distinctly heard footsteps on the stair. 'Gracious Heaven!' exclaimed she, in a whisper, 'there, I believe, is my father! What shall we do? For God's sake hide.' The approach of the devil would have been nothing to me in comparison to that of the old desperate ragamuffin, in the situation I then was, so in a moment I was below the bed, where I found things in bad order, and besides, very little room for me. She slid into her bed straight above me, covered herself with the sheets, and fell a sniffing, as if in the most profound sleep. 'What a delightful ingenious creature she is,' thought I to myself; 'now I shall hear now nicely she will bring us off.' The door of the room opened; but, as I judged, too softly to be opened by her father, and the steps came over the floor, apparently, with all the caution the walker was master of, though his skill was not exquisite in that most necessary acquirement in night-wooing. He came close to the bed-side, and tried, in vain for a long time, to waken the dear deceitful creature, who at length was pleased to awake with many smothered exclamations of astonishment and high resentment. At length I heard her say, 'Scott, is it you?' 'Yes, to be sure it is,' said he. 'For shame!' exclaimed she; 'how have you the impudence to come into a solitary girl's chamber at this time of night. I assure you, it is a freedom of which I will not admit; and therefore, if you wish that I should ever speak to you again, go away this instant without saying another word.' 'God save the king, Mary!' said he; 'What's the matter w'ye the night? just as ane was never here afore.' 'I beg you will take notice what you say, sir,' said she, 'and begone instantly, else I'll ring the bell.' 'You had better go away, friend,' thought I, 'and be thankful she has given you warning — she'll be as good as her word, and ring the bell with a vengeance.' 'Suffer me one moment to explain,' said the lover, in a most suppliant tone, for he seemed to know the danger of the ground on which he was treading. 'I will not suffer a word,' said she, 'from one who treats me in this manner. I'd have you to know your distance and keep it. If I am consulted, and choose to admit a gentleman to a private tete-a-tete, that is all very well. I hope I know what freedoms I should admit of in such cases, and what not. But I will not have my privacy intruded upon in this manner if you were a prince of the realm; and so, instantly I say, go about your business.'

'Well, upon my word, the girl speaks excellent good sense,' thought I; 'and I hope the fellow will go away. When he does, O how dearly I will caress the spirited, dear, ingenious creature!' 'Well, I must go away, since you insist on it,' said he. 'Ay, pray do,' said I to myself; 'the sooner the better.' 'But, as some excuse for my behaviour,' continued he, 'I must tell you before I go, that, as I set out for the English market on Monday, and cannot see you again for six or seven weeks, I came to take leave of you, and bid you good-bye for a little while. I intended to have wakened you in the way you prescribed; but finding the hall door open, which is not usual, I thought I would come in and awake you myself.' 'Well, you are very kind,' said she, 'and I am obliged to you; but you have done very wrong, therefore, pray, go away, as I have particular reasons for desiring your absence to-night.' 'And so have I, sir, if you please,' thought I. I think that at this time she had put out her arm to push him away from the side of the bed, for I heard him say, with evident symptoms of surprise, 'Bless me, Mary, you are dressed! In full dress too! — ruffled at hands and neck! Why are you sleeping with your clothes on? Oh! I see! I see! Yes, you have particular reasons for desiring my absence to-night indeed! You are waiting for some other lover, and have

left the door open for him. You need not deny it, for
the thing is perfectly evident. But I shall disappoint him
for once, for I will not go away to-night.' 'But, friend,'
thought I, 'could I but reach the handle of the bell at
the back of the bed, which perhaps is not impossible
from this situation, I should get you a dismissal you are
little dreaming of.' 'And will you indeed presume to
stay here without my approval?' said she; 'or dictate to
me about my lovers? Once you have me under control,
you may — leave me instantly.' 'Well, if you force me to
go away, I will watch him at the door.' 'Watch him
where you please, but you may watch in vain — leave
the room.' 'I never saw you so very cross as you are to-
night, my beloved Mary, and I am sorry for it, for I had
a great many things to talk to you about. But, if you will
but suffer me to remain five minutes, I protest I'll ask
no more, and I will then go quietly home, and neither
watch your door nor window.' 'Well, as you positively
promise to go away at the end of five minutes, I'll
indulge you for once; but suffer me to rise, for I do not
like to converse with a gentleman in this guise.' 'I do
not see any harm in it.' 'Perhaps not; nor do I think
there is much; but it looks so careless and indelicate
that I never can submit to it.'

She arose; and as there happened to be only one chair
in the room, they were obliged to sit down on the side
of the bed. The stock being higher than the matress, it
was impossible to sit on it; so, after all, they were
obliged to lean across the bed. I heard every word that
passed with distinctness, and as the lover declared that
he had things of great importance to say to her, I took
particular note of them, and shall here give the
conversation of a lover who had only five minutes to

spend with his mistress, and was not to see her again for two months.

'Well now, after all, we are lying upon the bed; so you might as well have remained where you were.'

'I do not think it half so bad to lean across a bed, as to lie at full length upon it.'

'A woman's whimsie!'

'Say that it is a whimsie: such whimsies as have no evil tendency you may grant us. But the truth is, that I disapprove of the whole system of wooing by night, and heartily wish it were out of fashion, which I am told it is in every district of the kingdom but this.'

'I hope it never will be out of fashion here.'

'And why, pray?'

'Because, in the first place, it is always so delightful.'

'Not always, friend,' thought I; 'if you were in my situation, you would feel otherwise.'

'And, in the next place, one hears his sweetheart's mind much more explicitly.'

'I am not sure of that, Mr Scott,' thought I.

'And, in the third and last place, all our fathers courted that way — our mothers were courted that way — every farmer's wife in the three shires has been courted in that way, save a few of a very late date, and I should be sorry to see such a good old established system exploded.'

'I have been always told these things, but I do not give credit to them.'

'They are, however, true. I have heard the matter disputed by some pretenders to refinement, and to that false delicacy for which the age is notorious; and I have heard it proved to my entire satisfaction, and many curious anecdotes besides, relating to it. Laird K — y of

Ch — k — t courted his lady many a night in the hay-mow of her father's cow-house, and she was wont to milk him a jug of sweet milk before he set out on his journey home. The Laird of S — n — e courted his lady in the woods by night, and sometimes among his father's growing corn, who accused him very much of the broadness of the lairs that he made; and he is one of the first landward lairds of the country. The reverend minister of K — m — l courted his wife in her mother's dairy, in the dark; and once in attempting to kiss her, his wig fell into a pail of milk, and was rendered useless. The old woman got a terrible fright with it, when about to skim the milk next morning. All the seven large farmers in the upper part of our parish courted their wives in their own bed-chambers; and I have heard one of them declare, that he found the task so delightful, that he drew it out as long as he could with any degree of decency. My father did the same, and so did yours; ask any of them, and they will tell you. And besides, is it not delightful, the confidence that it displays in the indelible virtue of daughters, sweethearts, &c.?'

'Say rather, the carelessness of their virtue that it displays. I know, from my own experience, that it is impossible for a girl who allows it not to be placed in some very disagreeable dilemmas.'

'Oh, you allude to your late adventure with Geordie Cochrane? Upon my word, you served him as he deserved! I never was so much pleased and diverted with any thing that ever I heard in my life.'

'Geordie Cochrane's very much obliged to you neighbour,' thought I; 'and he may, perhaps, live to be even with you yet.'

'Say not a word about Mr Cochrane, sir; for I will not

suffer one of my lovers to slander another of them to my face. When he comes back, he may possibly be as much inclined to talk about you.'

'Him! He speak of me! If he durst, I would claw the puppy-hide of him! He is as great a skype as I know of.'

I heard the little imp like to burst into laughter as he said this, and that all the while she was trying to stop him by holding her hand upon his mouth, for the sentences came out piecemeal and in vollies.

'I would rather see you married on any plowman, or — (bhoo — cease!) — tailor or weaver — (bhoo, give over I tell you) in the country. No man or woman can depend on a word he says, he's the greatest liar (bhoo-oo-oo)'

'D——n the fellow!' said I to myself, 'could I but reach the handle of the bell, I would astonish him.' I struggled all I could to reach it.

'What is that below the bed?' said he.

'It is our old dog Help, poor fellow, that I often keep with me to bear me company, and be a kind of guardian against intruders like you. Help, go away, you old slyboots; it behoves you well to lie there, and listen to all that passes between my lover and me.'

This gave me a little toleration to move, and I struggled more and more to reach the handle of the bell. I was almost smothered to death, while another was lying in the arms of my mistress; so I was determined to suffer the base intruder no longer. But all that I could do, I could not reach the handle of the bell, or rather I could not find it.

'Lie still, Help,' cried she, 'and be at peace; and I'll let you out in two minutes.' I thought I would suffer a little longer for the sake of her dear company; so,

wiping my dripping brows, I composed myself to my
state of sufferance as well as I could. The important
courtship of the lovers terminated here, and I heard,
from what they said, that they were greatly alarmed at
something they heard below. 'Merciful Heaven!'
exclaimed the lady; 'Who can it be? It is some one
speaking to my father in at the window!' I listened as
attentively as I could — they did the same — and at
length I heard the old farmer say, 'watch ye the door,
an' I'll gang up an' see what I can see.' 'Now friend,'
thought I, 'it is your turn come; and if you do not get it
I am mistaken.' He had just time to spring from the
bed, and shut himself into a corner press, before the
lady's father entered. Mary had hastily composed her
decent form on the bed, and pretended to be sound a
sleep. He came forward and with some difficulty
awaked her; while she seemed to be much frightened
and discomposed, and asked what he wanted? 'I want,'
said he, 'to see if there is any body with you.' 'Any body
with me, father! — what do you mean? You see there is
nobody here.' 'I dinna understand that, Miss. Aedie,
our herd, tells me, that he saw that silly profligate thing,
Geordie Cochrane, come riding this way after the
gloaming; and that his beast is standing tied at the back
\of the dike just now.'

'It is not likely he would come here after the last
reception he got; but take no notice of it, he will be with
some of the maids, and he'll go away as he came,' said
she.

'A fine story, faith! that he would be with ony o' the
maids, an' kens the gate here! deil tak' him, gin I catch
him here again hingin' o'er my bairn, like a hungry tod
o'er a weel nursed lamb, an' I dinna pu' the harrigalds

out o' him!' So saying, by a natural impulse, which led him to the only door that was in the room, except the one he entered by, he tried to open the door of the press; but it resisted his pull, although it was not quite close. When he found this, he made it come open with such fury, as if he would have pulled down the house, and there stood his old acquaintance Scott, staring him in the face like a hunted wild cat from its den. 'L——d have a care o' us!' said the old farmer; but, before he had time to articulate another word, the lover burst by him, and, running down stairs, made for the door. On the outside of the door there stood the staunch shepherd with his club, who, thinking it was me that was coming on him with such rapidity, determined to have a hearty blow at me, and no sooner did Mr Scott set his head out at the door, than he hit him on the links of the neck with such force, that he was laid flat on the gravel, and the shepherd above him with his knees and elbows. The old farmer followed, and I suspect that between the two Scott got but very rough treatment, for there was a terrible affray before the door for some time, and a great deal of oaths going. He must certainly have been hard put to it, for I heard him saying: 'If you wont let wooers come to see your daughter, d——n you, keep her and make a table-post of her. I'm as good as she, or any of her kin, ——d——n you; keep her, and make a tea-cannister of her, if you like.' 'A bonny story, faith!' said the old farmer.

I now began to drag myself out of my hole, anticipating the most delicious morning's courtship with my jewel that ever man enjoyed; but she begged me to lie still until I heard how matters settled, and regretted, as a pernicious business, the discovery made of my horse. I thought the old rascal could never once dream that there was another lover in the chamber, and therefore considered myself as perfectly safe. However, up he came again. 'Mary,' said he, 'the herd assures me that Cochrane is here.' And without waiting for any reply, he went to the press, and examined it more minutely; then, kneeling down on his hands and knees, he lifted the curtain and peeped beneath the bed. He did not speak a word on making the joyful discovery; but, observing where my feet lay, he set down the candle, hastened to the end of the bed, and, seizing me by the two feet, soon had me lying on my back on the middle of the floor.

'Deil pike out my een,' said he, 'gin ever I saw the like o' this sin' my mother bure me! Gude-faith, ye hae been playing at hide-an'-seek here! Chap, what think ye o' yoursel, now?'

'Whatever I may think of myself,' said I, 'it is apparent that I think more of some one else, that I have ventured so much for her.' 'Fine government, faith!' said he, while all the time holding me by the feet, with one on each side of him, so that I could not move, but lay on my back, and looked him in the face; and, for the first time, I perceived to my astonishment, that he seemed to watch Mary's eye for the regulation of his behaviour toward me. 'What say you to it, Miss? What have you to say for yourself?' 'I have nothing to say either for or against myself; but for the gentlemen, I must say that they are both gone mad.' 'Ay, and waur than mad!' cried he, encouraged by this remark of Mary's. 'It is a mischievous madness theirs. Ane creeps into ae corner, an' another into another, to watch a poor bit innocent sleeping lassie, and a' to be her ruin; it can be for nought else. May the ill thief be my landlord, chap, gin I dinna bury my fit in ye up to the instep.' I was still lying in the same posture as before — the most awkward one in which a lover could be introduced to his mistress's father, or herself either, and had no power to help or defend myself. Had he given me the kick he meditated, he had finished my course; but Mary raised her hand — which chained him still in a moment! 'Hold!' said she, 'let Mr Cochrane go; I want to speak with him.' He dropped my legs that instant, and I was not long in getting on my feet. 'What!' said he, 'and leave him here with you?' 'If you please, sir.' The old farmer, although he was in very bad humour, actually turned round at the first word, on purpose to leave me with his lovely daughter. I never was so much astonished in all my life.

'Humph!' said he, 'fine wark, faith! Od, dame, ye coudna stand this an' ye waur made o' bell-metal.'

'Speak, my dear father,' said she, softly — and he turned about.

'You know, though I am perfectly innocent of their coming here, yet were you to turn out Mr Cochrane now, it would expose me to the servants in a most ridiculous light, and actually ruin me. So, go away and deny that he is here. You surely are not afraid to leave me with any of them?' 'I'm nae fear't for ony imprudence, lassie; and I'm nae fear't ye *do* aught that's wrang; but it's your mind that I'm sad for; they'll gie't a wrang swee, thae chaps. Od, they'll pit ye daft! Weel, weel; ye may tak your crack there, sin it maun be sae.' And away he went, closed the door, and left us to improve the subject in any way we liked.

'Well, my dear Mary,' said I, standing like one

petrified, and in the dark, 'of all the things I ever witnessed this has surprised me the most; for I always imagined that your father tyrannized over you, and kept you in check, which made you the more willing to over-reach him when opportunity served.'

'You never were more deceived in your life, then,' said she; 'I am frequently obliged to make use of my father to expel those idle young gentlemen who come about me; often merely, as I suspect, to amuse themselves. He is proud of the trust; and often on such occasions assumes very high ground; but my will is his; and he has no wish but mine in such cases. I never expose my lovers to any insult from my father, unless for very good reasons; and I am sometimes driven to shifts to prevent them running their heads together; but I never yet conversed with a lover that I did not inform him of, as well as what I thought of the lover's motives in paying his addresses to me.'

'I stand on ticklish ground here,' thought I; 'therefore must take good care what I say or propose, in a case like this. As the sailor said to his captain, "No sham here, by G——." ' 'Mary,' said I, 'you astonish me still more! But was it not rather hard to give me such a passport out of the house, as you did that night?'

'No;' said she, 'I thought you deserved it. You might have observed, that whenever I desired you to stay all night, my father said no more, but talked to you as a welcome guest; and I thought you were wronging his hospitality, and infringing on the honour of his house, when you left your chamber without leave, and came into that of his daughter.'

'You are an extraordinary girl, Mary,' said I, 'and I can't approach you, even in the dark, but with a kind of fear and trembling. But, the devil! you did not tell him of the drop, surely?'

'Every thing concerning it. He knew you were in the house that night — and that you were in the garret; but did not choose to see you, till he knew if it was by my appointment.'

'I think,' said I, 'you may take for your motto, "Wha dare meddle wi' me." Pray, may I ask if it was by chance, or through design, that you gave me such a tumble from the window?'

She was again moved to irresistible laughter. 'I beg,' said she, 'that you will not mention that subject again, for I have many a time laughed at it already till nearly exhausted.'

'Upon my word, I'm very much obliged to you, Miss.'

'I meant to give you a slight fall; but not by half such a serious one. It was an accident that made me lose my hold at the first, and I was greatly alarmed till I saw you rise and run halting away; then I went to my bed, and laughed almost the remainder of the night. The awkward way that you fell, with your shoes rattling about your head — the astounded and ill-natured manner in which you rolled yourself over and over on the gravel — the length of time you sat considering, and, as I believed, cursing my slim fingers — the noise of dogs and men within doors, and the limping mode in which you made your escape, have altogether left such an impression of the ludicrous on my mind as shall never be erased. Never shall I see anything so exquisite again! Whenever I am down-hearted, I have only to think of that night to make me merry. I have gained a great deal of credit by it; for whenever I wish to laugh at the stories of any old prosing gentleman, or intolerable dowager, I think of your acute escape from my window, and laugh most unfeignedly, by which I have several times been praised as a most acute sensible girl.'

'It is a subject,' said I, 'on which I never felt any inclination to be merry; and when I furnish you with another divertisement, I sincerely hope it may be by some *less feeling* exhibition. I suspect that you are an exquisite wag.'

'I do not think the scene of this present night was much behind the other,' said she. 'Indeed, it is such a one that I dare not trust myself a moment to think about it; but, once I have the incidents all collated and arranged, I am sure I shall have many a hearty laugh at it. Being very lonely here, I like a little diversion with the fellows now and then.'

Afterwards we began a conversing about a Moffat ball that we had both been at, and about the various characters that were there, which served us for a topic of conversation until the time of my dismissal; and thus terminated two night-courtships, without a word of love. I was ashamed of this when I thought of it; for it was a neglect that never used to be the case with me; but I do not know how I was led away from the subject. I believe that girl could have led a man to converse on any subject, or kept him off any, she pleased. I left her with a much higher idea of her character than ever I had before, and was vexed that I had made such a poor use of the time so graciously afforded me.

But I am an unfortunate man; and my love affairs had not been to prosper; for hanging and marrying, they say, go by destiny. One would have thought that the favour shewn me by this lady, and the confidence reposed in me, both by herself and father, bespoke a preference in my favour. I thought so myself, and was very proud of it; not having the least doubt but that I could get my beloved Mary for the asking. How wofully was I mistaken! Just as I was contemplating another journey to see her, I received the following letter.

'Sir,

'I have taken into serious consideration your visiting here clandestinely, and sorely repent me for encouraging it. If I have judged aright of your motives, such visits may lead to evil, but can never lead to good; therefore, I beg that you will discontinue them. To convince you that I am serious, I must tell you, in confidence, that I have now promised my hand to another, who, if he has less merit, has more generosity than you, for he asked it.

'Your most obedient servant,   M.T.'

I read the letter twenty times over, and could scarcely believe my eyes. It cut me to the bone. I certainly had never asked her hand in marriage, nor even once mentioned the subject. She had taken it ill; but it was a subject that I never was very rash in proposing; for, in truth, it was not very convenient for me. My father and mother were both living in the same house with myself, and I had no separate establishment. However, I could not think of losing the dear creature, so I wrote a passionate love-letter, proposing marriage off-hand; and, after I had sent it away, I trembled for fear of its being accepted. However, the letter, though it had been opened and read, was returned to me, enclosed in a blank cover; so I found all chance of succeeding in that quarter was gone for ever. She was married to a young farmer on the December following.

The next time that I fell in love was at a Cameronian sacrament, with a tall, lovely, black-eyed girl, the most perfect picture of health and good-nature that I had ever seen. Her dress I could not comprehend, as it was rather too gaudy and fine for a farmer's daughter, and yet the bloom of her cheek bespoke her a country maiden. I watched her the whole day from the time that I first got my eyes upon her, and asked at every one I knew who she was; but no one could tell me. On such occasions, persons often meet whose places of abode are a hundred miles from each other; from such a distance round do they assemble to this striking and original exhibition. — For my own part, I would have enjoyed it very much, had it not been for this bewitching creature, who quite unhinged all my devotional feelings. There was scarcely a young man's eye in the congregation that was not often turned on her, for she had a very striking appearance. I could not help thinking that there was something light in her behaviour; but the liquid enamel of her black eye was irresistible, and I felt that I was fairly in love with I knew not whom. All that I could learn of her was, that some person called her *Jessy*; and I watched which way she went at even. I perceived, likewise, that she lived at a great distance, from the early hour at which she left the meeting. I could not get her out of my mind for days and months. I went to every kirk and market in the bounds toward which she went, but could neither see nor hear of her for upwards of eight months. At length I discovered her at a great hiring fair on the border the spring following.

I watched her the whole day as before, but having scarcely any acquaintances there, I had no means whatever of learning any thing about her rank, her name, or where she lived. About one o'clock, I chanced to meet with a gentleman who had often bought sheep from my father and myself, whose name was Mr John Murray of Baillie-hill, and whose company I loved very much. He proposed that we should dine together, to which I gladly consented. There was a Mr Bell and a Mr Moffat with us, both Eskdale gentlemen, whom I had never seen before; but they were both jolly, good-natured, honest fellows, and we plied the bottle rather freely. I got so much exhilarated by the drink, that I told them of being desperately in love with a girl that was in the fair, whom I did not know — that I had been in close pursuit of her for eight months — that it was in hopes of finding her that I came to the fair — and now that I had found her, I could in no way discover who she was. The gentlemen were highly amused, and every one gave me a different advice. Mr Bell bade me buy her a new gown for a fairing, and ask the direction to put on it. Mr Moffat bade me take time, and be cautious, and make some inquiries. 'Ay, d——n thee, Jock!' said the other, 'thou'lt take time, and be cautious, and make inquiries till thy head grow gray, an' thou'lt see the upshot.' There was a Mr Thomas Laidlaw came in, who gave me the strangest advice of all, but which cannot be repeated. At length my friend Mr Murray said, 'I tell thee, Geordie, lad, what I wad de mysale. I wad gae frankly up to the lass, and say, My bonny dow, I's fa'an in love wi' thee; an', feath, thou maun tell me wha thou is, an' I'll gie thee a kiss an' a braw new gown into the bargain.' The rest hurra'd, and approved of John's plan;

but I said it was impossible to do that, as it might give
the young lady offence. 'Offence!' said he, 'Domm thee,
gouk, dost thou think that a woman wul be offendit at
a chap for fa'ing in love wi' her? Nay, nay; an' that be a'
the skeel thou has, I gie thee up for a bad job. Thou
kens naething at a' about women, for that's the very
thing of a' ithers that they like best. An' thou offend
them wi' that, I little wat what thou'lt please them wi'.
Now, gie me thy hand, like a brave lad, an' promise that
thou'lt gae and de as I bid thee, an' thou'lt soon fin' out
wha she is, thou's tied to de that.'

All the rest applauded Mr Murray's plan with loud
huzzas; so I gave him my hand, and promised that I
would go and do as he had directed. Away I went, half
inebriated as I was, to put the scheme in execution,
while Mr Moffat cheered me out at the window. I soon
found her out; for though love be blind in some
respects, he is very sharp-sighted in others. — She had
just come out of a house with a party of borderers, utter
strangers to me, and who were taking leave of each
other. I went boldly into the midst of them, tapped the
girl on the shoulder, and when she turned round, said
familiarly, 'Miss Jessy, I want to speak a word with you
— I have a message for you — will you walk this way, if
you please?' She followed me without any hesitation
into a little area. 'You must not be astonished at what I
am going to tell you,' said I; 'for, in the first place, it is
simple, honest truth, which always deserves a hearing;
— I am in love with you — most violently and
passionately in love with you, and have been so for
these eight months.' I'll never forget the look that she
gave me — it was eloquence itself; the eloquence of
nature, and in a language that could not be mistaken. It

was something between fear and pity, and I am certain she thought I was deranged. 'I am not in jest, Jessy,' said I again; 'I never was more serious in my life: Ever since I saw you at D—f—e sacrament, I have been so overcome by your beauty, that I have neither had rest nor peace of mind, and I humbly beg that, for the future, we may be better acquainted.' 'Lad, I's rad thou's hardly theesel,' said she, in the true border twang; 'I never saw thei atween the eyne afore. I disna object nought at a' to thei acquaintance; but we canna be acquainted a' at ance.' 'If you are free to form an acquaintance with me, and willing to form it, that is all I desire, and all I request at present. Pray, have I your consent to pay you a visit?' 'I'se muckil obleyged to thei, sur; I'se shure I should leyke very weil to sey thei, an' seye, I daur say, wod mee feyther: — but thou canna be nought but jwoking a' this teyme.' 'I protest to you again, that I never was more serious in my life, which I hope to prove; for I am sure such a lovely face must be the index to a pure exalted mind, and a kind benevolent heart. Will you be so kind as give me the direction to your father's house? I am unacquainted with the roads thereabouts, and shall have hard finding it.' 'Oo! juost ower the sweyer there, and up the waiter till thou come to the boonmost town; that's auld Tammy Aitchison's. Than mee feyther's is the neist town ower the hill frey thei; juost speare for Robie Armstrong's at the Lang-hill-side-gate-end.' 'O, yes!' said I; 'I know now perfectly well. What, is this the name of old Thomas Aitchison's farm?' 'B——p——a, thou kens,' said she; 'Tammy an' I's well acquaintit; he'll like fine to see thei coming up the Hope.' 'Well,' said I, 'I'll come and see you in a fortnight, or twenty days at farthest;

but come, now, and let me buy your fairing.' She accompanied me to a craim, and I bade her choose a fancy gown. She again took a long, silent, and thoughtful look of me, measuring me from head to foot; and there was something quite new to me in all this. She looked at me with as much pride and innocence as a young colly-dog would look at its master. I could not think her vulgar; for a face so much indicative of health, love, and joy, I never looked upon; it was as fresh as a rose, and as delicate; but her frame was scarcely proportionate, being rather large, and, in some points too voluptuous. She remained silent, until I again desired her to make a choice; and then she absolutely declined accepting of any thing beyond the value of a ribbon, or a small buckling-comb, as a keepsake. It was in vain that I solicited; so I bought her a roll of ribbon, with which I presented her; but observing that she cast her eyes casually on a web of sarsnet, I bought a frock of it, and handed the merchant a direction where to send it. I perceived by this time that there were several good-looking, sunburnt, well-dressed, young men eyeing us all this while with more than ordinary earnestness; and I likewise observed, that Miss Armstrong was watching some one with a good deal of triumph in her eye. She was sitting on the end of the merchant's craim. 'Now, my angel, give me a kiss before we part, as an earnest of better acquaintance,' said I. 'Ay, that's right,' said the pedlar. This seemed to be a request that she wished, or at least expected, should be made, for she instantly turned round her beauteous face, elevating it with the simplicity of a child, and gave me what I asked, without either hesitation or confusion, save a slight blush, that gave her neck a little of the hue of the moss-rose. At that moment a gentleman came hastily forward, and, taking her by the hand, he led her away, without taking any notice of me. She made me a courtesy, however, and smiled to me over her shoulder. 'Ah, you have made some hearts sair this day!' said the peddling merchant. 'Did you see how the chaps were looking?' 'So you know Jessy, I see?' said I. 'Know her!' said he. 'Aye, and her father afore her. She's a sweet gipsy, it maun be confessed!' When I heard that, I looked my watch, and made off as fast as my feet would carry me. I had a mind to have asked a number of things at the pedlar, but when I heard that she was one of the gipsies, that I had been courting and kissing in the open fair, I thought I had heard enough for one time.

Afraid to face my friend, John Murray, and his associates, I sauntered about the street — went and got my father's mare corned, and had some thoughts of riding straight home, without ever looking back to the border again. The merchant observed me passing among the crowd, and beckoned me to him. 'Master,' said he in a whisper, 'tak' care o' yoursel. There was a wheen chaps here speerin after you, an' they're gaun to gie you a leatherin.' 'A leatherin, friend!' said I, 'pray what may that mean?' ' 'Tis what we ca' threshin' ane's skin i' some places; or, a drubbing, as an Englishman wad ca't,' returned he. 'They can have no hostility against me?' said I. 'Steelity here, steelity there, they're gaun to try't. They think nought o' that here-away. But they'll gie you fair play for your life. They canna bide that ye sude come an' snap away the bonny lass, an' the lass wi' the clink frae amang them.' I understood the meaning of this term well enough. I knew that this girl with whom I was madly in love, was beautiful, but now that I heard she had money I looked a little bolder, though how a gipsy should have a fortune I could not see. 'Well, well!' said I, 'let the blades come on, since that is the case; any one of them may perhaps meet with his man.'

'Nay, they'll gie you fair play,' said the pedlar. 'But gin ye let yoursel' be lickit, nouther the lass nor her father will ever look at ye or hear ye speak; you'll find that I tell you as a friend; an' thae Liddilhead devils are nae canny to cowe haffats wi.' I thanked him for his kindness; bade him take no concern about me; and, having got a hint that my captivator was rich, I thought that though she was come of the blood of the Egyptians, I would hie back to Mr Murray and his friends, and acquaint them with the success of my enterprise. At the same time I could not help wondering at what I had heard. I perceived that there was something in Border life, manners, and feeling, quite abstract from any thing I had ever witnessed before.

I found my friend, John Murray of Baillie-hill, and his jovial companions, still over the bowl, and in a high state of elevation. Mr Moffat arose, shook me by both hands — asked of my success, and said, he hoped I had done nothing rashly. As the rest were in a warm debate about the *crocks of Nether Cassway* and *the eild ewes of Billholm*, I sat down beside him, and related all my adventure with the young lady; but I still thought, from the want of speculation in his eye; that he was not taking me very well up; when I had done, I found that he did not comprehend, or rather did not recollect an item of what I had told him; so I was beginning to relate it all over again to him, for I liked the frank, unaffected manners of the gentleman exceedingly; but Mr Murray stopped me; 'Cuom, cuom,' said he, 'hae thee duone lad; Jock's ower far gane to take up thy story the night; an' thou wad tell him till the muorn at day light, thou'lt never make him either the dafter or the wiser.' 'Heard ye ever the like o' that?' said Moffat, 'to say that I canna take up a story? I can take up any story that ever was told in English. But I maun hear it first. I'll defy a man to take up a story before he hears it. Na na — that's impossible — you canna do that mair than I.' 'Woy dear man thou haurd it aw alraidy,' said Mr Bell, 'and yet thou disna mind a single sentence o't. I'll bet thee a bowl o' punch that thou disna tell o'er ae sentence of what Mr Cochrane tauld thee juost now about his sweetheart.' 'Done,' said the other, and the wager was taken; but when Moffat came to recite his sentence, he related distinctly enough the history I gave them before going out — his memory retained nothing later, and he vowed he had heard no more.

Murray, who was likewise half-seas-over, gave me the history of my border sweetheart, a subject of great interest to me. Her father was an old shepherd, a man who had been singular in his youth, both for strength and agility; and though only five feet seven in stature, a very diminutive size on the border, there was not one could cope with him, either at running, wrestling, or putting the stane. He added a very amusing anecdote of him, which was as follows.

His master, a Mr Jardine, betted twenty guineas with an English gentleman of the name of Whitaker, who declared that he never had been beat; that Armstrong would beat him at putting the stone; and they set a day on which Whitaker was to call at the shepherd's house, as by chance, along with two witnesses, and try the match. Jardine sent private word to his shepherd of what had taken place, and desired him to be at home on such a day; however, when the English gentleman called, he was not at home — there was none there but Meg Armstrong, his sister, who was busy up and down the house, baking bread, and churning the milk, &c. They asked very particularly about her brother, but Meg assured them he would not be home either that day or next, and begged if she might ask what they wanted with him? Whitaker said it was a matter of no consequence — a mere frolic — That he and his two friends had come off their way a little to see him, having heard so much of his uncommon strength, and that they intended to have tried him at putting the stone, and wrestling. 'Ay, ay,' said Meg, 'Weel I wot, sur, neything wod hae pleysed him better, had he been at heame — he's aftner at theye theyngs nor his beuk. But I trow aye he's neye grit stecks at them eftir aw, for I hae seyne the deye whon I cwod bett him an Jwock beath, but they hae gwotten queyte aheid o' me for a year or tway bygane, an' I tak it nae that weile out.'

Whitaker's friends thought this was high game, and instantly proposed that Meg Armstrong and he should try it, as a specimen of what her brother could do.

'I'll let thee see how fer I can throw it meesail, wi' aw my hairt,' said Meg; 'an yeance I faund the weight o' thei stane, I'll tell thei till a tryfle whithur thou or Robie will ding.'

They went out to an old green turf dike, where it was apparent that much of the business of putting had been going on, as there were choice stones of every dimension lying about, and the ground so beat up, that there was not a blade of grass upon it. Meg bade him choose his stone. He chose one about twenty pounds weight, and threw it carelessly, not thinking it necessary to exert himself to beat a woman. Meg then took up the stone, and throwing it as carelessly, and with as much apparent ease, sent it full two yards beyond him. The Englishmen damned themselves if ever they saw the like of that! and it was not until he stripped off his coat and boots, and threw it six times, that he was able to break ground before Meg, which at last he did. Meg tucked up the sleeves of her short-gown; and, taking up the stone again, threw it with so much art, that it went a foot and a half beyond Whitaker's mark. The latter tried it again twice, but not being able to mend his last throw an inch, he gave in with good humour; but he was quite convinced in his own mind that Meg was a witch. Whitaker was nearly six feet and a half high, and Meg could almost have stood under his arm.

'Thou's naething of a putter,' said Meg, 'I see by the way thou raises the stane; an thou saw my billy Rwob putt, he wad send it till here. Now, an thou likes, I'll try thee a warstle te; for I comes nearer till him in that nor ony theyng else.'

Whitaker would not risk his credit with Meg a second time, as he had no doubt of the issue; but, giving her a guinea, he shook hands with her, and went his way. Shortly after this he enclosed the amount of his wager, and sent it to Mr Jardine in a note, intimating, that he had missed his shepherd when he called; but was fully convinced, from some accounts he had heard of him, that he would have been beat.

The secret never was acknowledged, but every one acquainted with the family knew, that Meg Armstrong, Rob's sister, who was a sprightly handsome girl, fond of dancing and dress, never could wrestle a fall with an ordinary man in her life, or putt a stone; nor did she ever attempt either, save on that occasion. There was therefore no doubt, but that Rob had sent his sister out to the hills to tend the sheep that day, and had dressed himself in her clothes, in order that he might not be affronted if the Englishman beat him, and to humble his antagonist as much as he could.

Mr Murray having told me of this exploit of my intended father-in-law at this time, I thought proper to set it down here, as somewhat illustrative of a character which I had afterwards to do with. Of my border flower he told me, that she was an only daughter by a second marriage; that a maternal uncle of hers, who had been an under-clerk in a counting-house in Liverpool, and by a long life of parsimony had amassed a considerable fortune, had left her his sole heiress, so that the girl had of late been raised to move in a sphere to which she had not been bred; and that her personal beauty, simplicity, with the reports of her great fortune, had brought all the youths on the border to her as wooers. 'An' I can juost tell thee, lad,' added Mr Murray, 'afore thou gets away Jainny, thou'lt hae ilka wight chap to fight atween the head o' Liddal an' the fit of Cannobie.' 'I have got some short hints of that already,' said I; 'but tell me, my dear friend, has she got none of the blood of the gipsies in her; for her bright black eyes and long eye-lashes bring me very much in mind of a young Egyptian?' He laughed at me, and said I was raving. 'The deil a drap of gipsy blood's in her veins!' said he. 'Her mwother was ane o' the Pairks o' the Woofcleuchead, and her feyther's ane o' the true auld border Armstrangs.' I then confessed to him, that I heard a merchant at a craim say she was a gipsy. 'Oh!' said he, 'that's been Pether Willie o' Hawick. A' the women are gipsies wi' him. He never ca's ane o' them by another name. He gies my daughters ney other titles, juost afwore my feace, than gipsy Jean and gipsy Nannie.'

At that instant there was a tall raw-boned fellow, with a gray plaid tied round his waist, who opened the door and looked in, without accosting any of the company; but I perceived that he looked very eagerly at me, as if examining my features and proportions with wonderful curiosity. He closed the door quietly, and went away; but, in about ten minutes afterwards, he opened it again, and inspected the company in the same way as before. 'What the devil do you want, sir?' cried Mr Moffat furiously, who was by this time nearly whole-seas over. 'Ney aill te thei ata', mon; haud thei gollaring tongue,' said the fellow, and closed the door. About two minutes after, another handsome, athletic, well-dressed borderer, opened the door, and surveyed our party. 'What the devil do you want, sir?' cried Mr Moffat. The man hastened out, and closed the door; but I overheard him saying to his associates, 'That's juost the very mon; we hae him seafe and snwog.' 'By G——,' said Murray; 'these are the chaps alraidy watching to hae a bellandine wi' thee — an thou tak nae guod caire, lad, thou's in cwotty Wollie's hands. I ken the faces o' them weel — they canna leave a fair without some strow, an' they're makin thee their mark the neyght. Thou maunna steer frae this board; an' then, when it grows mworning, we'll a' munt an' ride away thegither.' I confess, when I overheard what the fellow said on closing the door, and this suggestion of my friend's, I felt a thrilling apprehension, which made me very uneasy; however, I pretended to treat the subject lightly; and, like all other young puppies, my boastings and threatenings of the other party were proportionate to my fears of them; for I swore I would make an example of the first that presumed to intrude his snout into our company again. Mr Moffat applauded my resolution, and out-swore me, saying that he would do the same. He even went farther, for he swore he would fight them all, one after another.

'Thou'lt fight the devil!' said Mr Bell, who seemed to have a great friendship for Moffat, and an anxious wish to keep him from any unwarrantable sally; 'thou'lt fight wi' the devil, Jwock! I tell thee, keep thy seat and be quiet. Thou'lt nae quorrel nor fight wi' a human creature till thou be that way thou canna stand thy leane, and then thou wad quorrel wi' the cat an she wod quorrel wi' thee.'

Moffat, however, brooding on the insult we had suffered, in being intruded and stared on by blackguards, as he supposed them to be, proposed to me, by way of retaliation, that we should open their door thrice, inspecting them in the same manner, and see how they liked it; and the more his friends disapproved of it, the more intent he grew of putting his scheme in execution. I could not well refuse to accompany him, as it was I who began the bragging, though I did not inwardly approve of the measure, from its being so like seeking a mischief. However, away we went at last, in spite of all our friends could say to us, and opened the door of a large ballroom, stood in the door, and stared at the company, which consisted of about eight or nine countrymen, who were sitting in one of the corners over a bowl of smoking whisky-toddy. Just as we were going away triumphant, several of the company cheered Mr Moffat as an old welcome acquaintance, and called on him to drink their healths in a glass of toddy before he went. He made no hesitation in complying with this request, for he was in the humour to have done any thing, either good or evil; and, as his arm was linked in mine, we were instantly seated at the table among these wild borderers. 'Here's te thei, Mr Moffat,' said the tall athletic fellow that first opened our door. I could not help noting him particularly: He had large hands and prodigious wrists — fair lank hair of a bright yellow — a large mouth, and fresh rosy complexion. ' I say, here's te thei, Moffat, mon,' repeated he; 'thank ye, sir, said Mr Moffat; but wha am I to thank? for, faith, I hae forgot.' 'I's Tommy Potts i' the Pease-Gill, disnae thou meynd me?' 'O aye, I mind now,' said Moffat, 'was not it you wha ran at the wedding o' Dews-lees wantin' the breeks?' 'Ay, the very seame, Mr Moffat, thei memory's better than thei judgment after a'. ' Moffat was going to be in a great rage at this compliment, but another diverted his attention by saying, in a kind ardent voice, 'Mr Moffat, I's devilish glad to see thy feace, mon; here's te thei very guod health.' 'Thank ye, sir, thank ye,' said Moffat, looking stedfastly across the table; 'an' wha the devil are ye, for my memory's never unco clear in a fair-night?' 'I's Davie's Will o' Stanger-side, mon. I yeance coft thei crocks an' thei paulies, an' tou guidit me like a gentleman, else I had been hard pingled wi' them — Here's to thei, sir.' 'Here's thei guod health, Mr

Moffat,' cried a third; 'tou'lt hae fargot me too? I's Jock Hogg i' Mangerton.' 'Ay! Jock, is this you, man? Here's your health. Ye're the saftest chap ever I stude a market wi'.' 'And, Mr Moffat,' continued Jock Hogg, 'dis tou meynd Willie Elliot o' Weirhope-Dodd?' 'Mind Willie Elliot!' said Moffat, 'Ey, my faith, I'll no soon forget him! he's the greatest leear that ever I met wi' o' the race o' Adam.' 'Woy, this is him on my reyght hand,' said Jock Hogg, like to burst with laughter. Moffat never regarded, but went round inquiring all their names; and when he had done, he immediately commenced again. He was so well liked and respected by every body, that no one took offence at what he said, though he certainly gave great occasion.

At length Tommy Potts set his broad-blooming face across the table and accosted me nearly in these terms:

'Sae it seyms tou's coming to teake away Jaissy Armstrang frae amang us, wi' the pockfu' o' auld nails, an' aw thegither? Tou'lt be the lucky chap an' tou gets her. But I's rade, that auld Robie will think tou's hardly beane for her. I can tail thei, that he'll never gie her till a lad that canny carry her through the burn, an' ower the peat-knowe, aneath his oxter, an' she's nae wother-weight nouther. What says tou to that? I doubt tou'lt ne'er be beane for Jainny.'

I did not like the homeliness of this address; but, as I had seen a good deal of the same kind of manners during the day, I thought I would parry as good-humouredly as possible; so I said, I did not know the distance which the old man had set for the lover to carry his daughter, but that I certainly would exert my utmost efforts to gain such a lovely girl.

'Ney, ney,' said he again; 'I's shoor tou's nae beane

for Jainny. But, an tou haes a good genteel down-sitting for the lassie, auld Robie woll maybe discount thei a tetherlength or tway. Pray, is nae tou a tailor to thy business?'

'A tailor, sir!' 'Ay, to be shoor, a tailor.' 'A tailor, sir! what do you mean by that?' 'I ax your pardon, sir; I was only speerin' if tou was a tailor. I thought by thei dress tou mightst be a Moffat tailor; an' what o' that? I's shoor I hae seen a tailor a better mon than thei.'

'I would have you know, sir' said I, 'that I am not accustomed to such language as this; and, moreover, if I thought there was a better man in all your country than myself, I would blow out my brains.'

'Ney, ney; I ax your pardon, lad; what can a man de mair? I didnae mean to set thei on thei heich horse a' at yeans this geate; but we're noor unco nice o' what we say here, for we're aye content to stand by the consequences.'

'And, pray, does the consequence never occur, that a vulgar, impertinent scoundrel, such as you, who takes upon him to insult any stranger that comes into the company, should get himself kicked out of doors?'

'Woy, an the chap be fit te de it, the twother mawn bide by the consequences; there's nae law here but jwost that the thickest skin stands laungest out; and that tou'lt find, or tou taikes Jaissy Armstrang ower Sowerby Hap.'

'It is not me you have insulted, you have insulted the company, and your country too, by the manner you have spoken to me. I merely came in as Mr Moffat's friend, in good fellowship, and must insist on your leaving the room.'

'Ney, ney, I'll nae leave the room neyther.' 'But you

shall leave the room, sir,' said Mr Moffat, who had only heard the last two sentences, the mention of his own name having drawn his attention from a violent dispute he had got into with another man, about some tups, that Moffat averred were half muggs, and which the other man as strenuously denied. Potts, finding that the sentiments of the party, or at least the *voice* of the company in general, were against him for the present, succumbed a little, but apparently in very bad humour.

'Gointlemen, I's very sorry,' said he, 'for having offended the chop. I dwodna ken but what he could taike a jwoke an' gie a jwoke, like our nain kind o' lads; but I ax his pardon. What can a man de mair? I ax his pardon.'

'O, that's quite sufficient,' said Mr Moffat and the rest of the party — so Potts and I at length shook hands across the table. Mr Moffat and his opponent again began to their dispute about the breed of Captain Maxwell's tups; the rest fell into committees of a similar nature, according to their various occupations and concerns. Tommy Potts sat for a considerable time silent, leaning his temple upon his hand, and his elbow on the table, while his short upper-lip, which was nearly a span in length from cheek to cheek, seemed curled up almost to his nose, and his white eye-brows sunk fairly in below the arch of the eye, and pointed downwards. He was visibly labouring under a savage displeasure. At length he addressed me again as follows:

'But efter a', mon, I wasna jwoking thei about auld Robie an' his douchter. He was a very straung chop the sel o' him, and he has taukt about it a' his life, and about naithing else; an' it is the only quality that he cares a doit about in a man. If ever tou gaungs to court the

lassie, as I hae deune mony a time, tou maun first thraw
a' the wooers that are there at a worstle, or the deil a
word tou gets o' her. I hae been five times there mysel',
an' the shame fa' me an ever I guot a neyght's courting
yet; for I was aye turned up, an' obliged to come me
weys wi' me finger i' me mouth.'

'I was so much amused by this picture, and the way in
which it was described, that I laughed heartily at it, and
again got into free conversation with Potts. He assured
me that every word of it was truth; and added many
anecdotes of scenes that he had witnessed there and
heard of from others. 'An' be the bye,' added he, 'an
tou'lt worstle a fa' wi' I, tou sal kean what chaunce tou
hess; for I hae found the backsprents o' the maist part
of a' the wooers she hes.'

I was rather glad of this proposal, for I wanted to give
Potts his weight on the floor, and I felt confidently sure
of throwing him; for I had the art of giving a trip with
the left heel, which I never in my life saw fail with any
one that did not know the trick. However, I took care
never to wrestle with a man above once or twice; for
when my plan was once discovered, it was easily
avoided; and, as I trusted solely to it, I run a chance of
coming off with the worse. The ball-room, where we
were, was remarkably large, so that we had plenty of
room; and up we got, in perfect good-humour,
apparently, to try a fair wrestle, to the infinite delight of
the company. Potts was a tremendous fellow for bone. I
was afraid I would not be able to bring in his back close
enough to get a fair trip at his right foot. But this being
a manoeuvre that no wrestler ever suspects, in working
himself round with his side toward me, he brought
himself into the very position I wanted; for he meant to

throw me over his right knee. Quite sure of him then, I watched my opportunity; and the next moment, while he was in the act of moving the right foot a little nearer me, I struck it with my heel across before his left one, which brought him down below me with such freedom on the boards (for there was no carpet), that it was some minutes before he could speak. Every one present uttered some exclamation of astonishment, as no one had anticipated the issue but myself. Potts rose, drank off two or three glasses of toddy, changed colour as often, and sat down again much the same man as he was before; surly, savage, and dissatisfied.

'I never saw thei as easily thrawn ower in me life, Tommy,' said one. 'I trowed he wod hae studden the gentleman a better shake,' said another. 'He fauldit him like a clout,' said Mr Moffat. 'Weel, weel, gentlemen,' said Potts, 'the chop thrawed me, there's ney doubt on't; an' he thrawed me very fairly too; I's nae disputing't; but I'll bet a choppin wi' ony o' ye, that he'll be ney langer wi' the neist he tries than he was wi' mey, if the chop be willing the sel o' him.'

I said I was willing to risk a fall with any man, in good fellowship; and never hesitated on such matters. There was no one thought proper to accept my challenge; and, in consequence of my victory over Potts, and this acknowledged superiority, together with the fumes of the whisky-toddy, which high-mettled liquor we had imbibed with considerable liberality, I dare say I assumed rather too much for a stranger, and put on airs that scarcely became me, and which I would not have practised among intimate associates. But thinking I was landed in the company of a set of braggadocios, I resolved to abate no item of my dignity. Potts discovered this; and, still smarting from his late defeat, as well as for having been snubbed by the company before on my account, he made another effort to humble me, taking an opportunity while all the rest were loudly engaged in different disputes, so that no notice might be taken of it. We still filled the seats that we first occupied, straight opposite to each other, on different sides of the narrow board; when, in a half-suppressed voice of the most malevolent accent, he addressed me as follows:

'Tou hess thrawn me, there's nae doubt on't; an' tou's deune it fair eneuch. But what is there in that? tou hess nae right ava to coom into a coontry, an' brag thysel to be the best man in it, as I heard thee de the night; for I can tell thee, that tou's devilishly fer out o' the reckoning, for tou's naething but a dud to mony o' the chops o' this coontry. Thou took't sae ill to be thought a tailor; but, mon, I knows a tailor in this country that wod stap thei neb in a part o' thei — that I's no gaun to neame.'

Without answering him a word, I lifted the tumbler of toddy and threw it in his face, sending the glass after it with all my might. This last missile had probably finished the redoubted Tommy Potts for ever, had he not half warded it with his arm, which he dashed to his eyes as they smarted with the warm liquor. It however cut the bridge of his nose, which spouted blood. There was no room for interference now, and none attempted it. Potts loosed his neckcloth, and stripped off his clothes, saying all the while, 'Ey, mon, but thou's reather a shairp ane; but meynd the, that's a baptism that we border chops never teakes for neything. Tou maun fallow up the smack wi' something better nor that, or tou had'st better hae keepit it nearer theisel.'

I did not strip, being lightly clad, but met my antagonist in the middle of the floor as he advanced, and saluted him with a hearty blow on the left temple, which he returned, and we then instantly closed. I threw him, and gave him his own weight and my own right freely, but instantly jumped up and let him rise again to his feet, which I needed not to have done, for the border laws of war, as I was afterwards told, required no such thing, for 'The thickest skin stand langest out;' and they have no other. I was too late in being aware of this, else I might have saved myself from a great deal of trouble. He was a great deal stronger than I was — clumsy and raw-boned — with longer arms, and a heavier hand, but he was not so agile. Three times, in the heat of our scuffle, we closed, and every time I fell above him. One of these falls cut his wind considerably, for I had fairly the advantage for some time in striking, and mauled and disfigured his face most dreadfully; but he now took care, with his long arms, that we should not come to close gripes. I judged this to be all his aim, and therefore fought fearlessly, though with little science. He was master of a much more deadly art than throwing his antagonist in a struggle, and for that he had till now been watching. It was an open trip with the left foot, followed up by a blow with the right hand on the chest or face; and this he now practised on me so successfully, that I staggered to the further end of the room, and fell with my back against the wall. I felt a little stunned and giddy, but advanced with great rapidity again to the charge. I had now the worst of it; in four seconds he repeated his trip, accompanied with a tremendous blow on the brow, which made me fall freely back, and my head or shoulders striking on one of the forms, I lay in a state of utter insensibility.

It was long before I came to my senses, and then I found myself lying in a bed, with a surgeon and the mistress of the inn standing over me. Mr M—, the surgeon, had bled me copiously in both arms, and for a long time was in a state that I cannot describe; but felt excessively happy, and always inclined to laugh, yet so weak as not to be able to sit up in the bed. The surgeon left me, and ordered quietness; but what quietness can be had in the inn of a country town on the morning after a fair. About day-light, several of my evening associates came staggering and drowsy into the room, to inquire how I was before they went away, and among the rest, to my utter astonishment, in came Tommy Potts, with his face all patched and blotted, and the blood crusted in dark stripes from his brow to his toes. He came freely forward, and sat down on my bed-side, as if he had been a brother or a most intimate friend, looked anxious like to my face, and addressed me as follows, without ever giving me time to speak a word — fearing, I suppose, that my answers would be ill-natured.

'How is tou now, lad? Guod I's unco glad that tou's come about again, for I was rad that tou had left us awtegeather. I hae nae gatten sickan a gluff sen I was christened, (the first time I mean) an, be me certy, I was reather woshing it had been the sel o' me. Gie me thee hand, mon. I houp thou's nae the woar, an' we'll ay ken ane anwother again. Tou's as guod a chop to thee inches as ever I foregathered wi'. But ton maun never gang to brag a hale country-side again. An' yet after aw,

G–, tou fught devilish weel. An' I'll tell Jaissy that tou did. But tou hest crackit they credit there. But I'll tell her the truth; for, G –, tou did fight *devilish* weel.'

And with that Tommy Potts left me, in excellent humour with himself, with me, and with all the world; a state to which victory often influences our minds, while misfortune sours them in a proportionate degree. Mine was so. I was very unhappy, and greatly ashamed of the business; for there were so many who saw it, that it spread like wildfire, and made a great noise among the country gossips. It was some days before I could ride home, and after I got home, it was a good while before I could be seen.

This I did not much regard; for my mind was too much occupied with other matters to feel any regret for the want of the society of my country neighbours. These twenty days form the great era of my *love adventures*, and it was the only period in which I could be said to be *over head and ears in love*. I then cared for nothing else, thought of nothing else, and dreamed of nothing else, save that rural Border flower. It was like witchcraft — a spell by which I was bound I wist not how. I lost my appetite, and all delight in my loved field sports, and became a moping, languid fool, as bad as a greensick girl. I laugh to this day, when I reflect on the state to which I was reduced. I often caught myself, while repeating her name without intermission, an occupation which I perhaps had been following out with great assiduity for an hour or two — 'Jessy Armstrong! Jessy Armstrong! dear, dear, sweet, lovely Jessie Armstrong!'

This is no exaggerated account; for, on the contrary,

I felt ten times more than I can possibly describe. To such a loving disposition did this overpowering passion influence me, that I fell in love with other two, besides my adorable borderer. The one was a homely squat servant girl, in the neighbourhood, who chanced to have a cast in her eye that somewhat resembled Miss Armstrong's, or that I fancied resembled it, which amounted to the same thing, and I walked every day to get a blink of this divine creature's eye! The other was an old wife of the same hamlet, who spoke the border dialect in all its primitive broadness and vulgarity, which I thought the sweetest dialect on earth, and that there was a doric softness in the tones that melted the very heart: so I went every day to hear this delightful old wife speak! It must certainly be owing to some feelings that I then imbibed, that, to this day, I like better to hear that language spoken, than any other dialect in Britain.

I had said to this idol of my heart, that I would see her in three weeks at farthest. The time was nearly expired, and away I set on foot, a distance of fifty miles at least, to pay my addresses to her, not only burning and raving with love, but resolved to offer myself as a lover and husband, on any terms she chose. 'Give me but the simple, the beautiful, blooming Jessy Armstrong,' cried I, 'and I ask no more in life!'

The way was long and mountainous, but I took a good part of two days to walk it, being resolved to arrive there in the evening. I liked always night-courting best myself, having been as it were bred to it; and I never had any doubt, whatever some of the women might pretend, but that they too gave it the preference. At all events, I knew that in the sphere in which Miss Armstrong had been bred, in the shepherd's cot, namely, any other time would have been viewed as a practical joke. I asked always the road for B——p——a, the name of Mr Aitchison's farm; but, when I came there about the fall of the evening, I liked very ill to ask the road to Lang-hill-side-gate-end — I could not do it; so I was obliged to guess, and take the hills at random. It grew late — I lost all traces of a road — and was in no doubt but that I had gone astray, and would never reach the Lang-hill-side-gate-end by that rout. At length I came to a shepherd's cottage, into which I determined to go and ask the way, whatever shame it might cost me. I never thought any shame to go and court a bonny lass, but I could not endure that people should think I was come so far to catch a girl's fortune. However, in I went to ask the road, and found a group such as is often found in a shepherd's house, sitting round a hearth fire. It consisted of an old man, sitting on a bench made of dried ryegrass divots — his wife, a middle-aged woman, was sitting right opposite to him on the other side, carding fine wool on a pair of singularly long wool-cards — a young man, dressed in his sunday-clothes, with his plaid hung gracefully over the left shoulder, bespeaking him a stranger, sat on a chair before the fire; and a girl leaned with one knee on the hearth beside him, busily employed in lighting birns on the fire, and preparing the family's supper. I addressed them in the usual way, bidding them goode'en; which was repeated by them in rather a careless indifferent way, very unlike the kind bustle of hospitality that always welcomes a stranger in the house of a Scottish shepherd. I added the common and acute remark, that it was a fine evening. 'Aye, I's shure the e'ening's weel eneuch,' said the old shepherd. 'Are ye gaun a lang gate this wey the neight?' 'Upon my word,' said I, 'that is more than I well know. What may the name of this place be?' 'I dosna ken what it may be sometime or wother,' said he; 'but I kens weel eneuch what it's ca't juost now.' 'And, pray, what is it called just now?' said I. 'It's ca't be a neame that thou canst nae saye; sey thou wadna be ney the better an thou haurd it,' said the carl, in a tone, however, in which there was no ill-nature, but rather a kind of homely waggery.

By this time the girl had stirred up the blaze to a bright flame; and, throwing her ringlets back over her left shoulder, turned round her head and looked full at me. Good heavens! who was it, but my dear Jessy Armstrong? I was not only surprised, but perfectly confounded; for, of all things in the world, I least expected to find a lady with a fortune of a thousand pounds, or as some said of five thousand, in a lonely shepherd's cot; and I could not help feeling as if I had got into a scrape. It was so unlike the places to which I had formerly gone a wooing. 'Bless me, Miss Armstrong,' I exclaimed, 'is this you? I just stepped in to inquire the road to your place of residence, not thinking I would have the happiness to get to it so soon.' During this short speech, she blushed, turned pale, and blushed again, but made no reply. I had seized her hand, which she still suffered me to hold. 'I am so happy to see you again!' continued I; 'How do you do? I hope I find you well?'

'Trouth ey, I's weel eneuch. How's tou theesel?' replied she, still looking particularly embarrassed. But after I had replied to this, she plucked up a little

confidence, and said, 'Say thou hess fund thee way into
this coontry? I trowed ay thou wast jucking me; but
they say better leate threyve than ne'er de weel. Come
thee ways this waye, an' thraw fraebout thee plaid;
thou's welcome to the Lang-hill-side-gate-end for
aince.' So saying, she led me round the hallan — took
my plaid from me, and hung it up, at the same time
whispering into my ear, 'For thee life o' thee, denna tell
them who thou is; but ca' theesel some wother neame;
an' be sure to man theesel.' I could in nowise
comprehend the meaning of either of these injunctions;
but had not a moment's time to ask the explanation of
them, for we were now beside the company, and in a
moment she had set a seat for me, which she requested
me to occupy. I durst not speak a word, as I had some
new character to support, of which I had never
thought; and I blamed in my heart the caprices of
women, who are always inclined to throw a mystery
over every thing, and keep all concerned with them in
the dark as far as possible. So there I sat, scratching with
my nails at some spots of mud that had jerked on my
pantaloons, while the old man surveyed my limbs and
muscular frame with considerable attention. The wife
looked at me, as if she would have looked me through;
and the young shepherd, biting his lip, cast a malicious
and prying glance at me occasionally. We were all
embarrassed, and no one knew either what to do or say,
except the old wife, who again fell to her carding; the
young shepherd made figures with the end of his staff
among the ashes on the hearth, and Jessy walked about
the floor with a most elegant thousand pound air. The
old man was the first to break silence. 'Hess thou
comed fer the day, lad?' said he. I answered that I had

only come from Sorbie. 'Ey ey,' said he, 'dis thou ken
Sandy o' Sorbie? he's a gayan' neyce chap, Sandy; I yince
herdit to the feyther o'm.' 'Feyther,' said the malicious
and incomprehensible beauty, 'thou'lt no ken this lad?
He an' I's fa'n acqueant at the public pleaces. This is
Sandy Welch o' the Braeside.' 'Deed I kens noucht
about him, Jainny. I hae seen some o' thae Welches at
Staigshawbank mony a time, an' I's rad there's no that
muckle in them; for I never saw ane o' them owther
brik a chop's head, or take him be the neck, aw me
days.' I said, that though none of the Welches of *my*
family, would probably be the first aggressors in a
brawl, yet there were some of them, whose heads the
best men in the kingdom durst not break. 'Ey, trouth,
that may be, lad. I should lyke to see them. Hess tou
brought ony o' thae wi' thee?' 'No,' said I, 'I have come
by myself. I am one, I believe, of the weakliest of the
name, but I do not think I have seen a man, since I came
from home, that durst break my head.' 'Ey ey!' said he,
'dost thou say sae? Come, gie me thee hand; thou's a
chop o' some mettle eftir aw. An' is tou come to court
our Jainny?' 'That is rather a home question friend,'
said I. 'Ney, ney, it's a very fair question,' said he. 'I's no
saying tou's no to court her; thy reyght's as gwod as
anwother's. I's only asking, if thou is come to court.' I
was obliged to acknowledge, that I did come with the
intention of paying my addresses to his daughter.

'Then Wullie, lad,' said he, with a joyful
countenance, and looking to the young shepherd, 'thou
maun stand to thy taickle again.' The shepherd looked
offended, and said, 'It is very unfair; now when I have
turned up five already, and got so many strait grips, can
you think there's any justice in bringing a fresh man in

on me. I have set off five *already*, let him wait his day.'

I could not comprehend this; and did not yet believe, that what Tommy Potts told me, about the lovers wrestling for the maid's company, had any foundation in truth. The old shepherd, however, soon explained the matter.

'I dusna ken, Wullie Glendinning,' said he; 'thou may think it's hard for thee; but, yince a chop has made a reule, I see ney oose in brikkin through't. Thou canna beath hae the lass's company at the seame time, an' I wod reather see her wi' the better chop than wi' the wauffest o' the tway. I'll tell thee what it is, Sandy Welch; sen ever my Jainny got a claut o' gear, the lads are like to pu' others thrapples out about her; an' when twey or threy o' them come in ae night, as they will ay aw be rinning on a Friday night, an' aw the saum gate, we juost gar them try a werstle; an' whae-ever coups the lave, we let him try his hand at the courtin' for a wey, an' the rest maun jwost strodd their ways. The lassie has walth o' gear to maintain baeth the sel o' her, an' ony chop she likes to marry, and whin that's the case, I wod reather that she got a man than a bauchle.'

'It is a singular way of casting lots for a proper husband, indeed,' said I, 'and worthy of a Border sheil. But, pray, does Miss Armstrong herself perfectly acquiesce in this plan?'

'Bless the heart o' thee!' said he; 'she's the strickest o' the hale twote. She'll no bate a fallow an inch, if he war the son of a luord. Very little wod hae meade my Jainny a man, for she wants neane o' the spirit o' ane.'

'I know nothing of the art of wrestling,' said I, 'but for the sake of your daughter's company, I'll stand the test at that or any thing else.'

'Deil a bit, but thou's a lad o' some spunk,' said he; 'an' thou's better beane than Wullie Glendinning, but he pretends to be a master o' the art. Coom coom, Jainny, lassie, tak thou the bouet an' gie me a candle, I'll haud it i' the bung o' me bonnet, an we'll see some mair fine sport.'

Miss Jessy was not slack, she lighted a candle and put it into a lantern, which she called a bouet, and gave another candle to her father, who kept it burning by holding it knowingly in the lee side of his bonnet; and out we went to a beautiful green level, and stripped off our coats and shoes, to wrestle for a night's courting of this beautiful rural heiress. I pretended great ignorance, and made as though I did not even know how to take my hold. Miss Jessy directed us, determined to see fair play, and as soon as we were rightly placed for action, I fell a struggling, with as much awkwardness as I could assume, until both my antagonist and the old man laughed outright at me, for ever attempting to wrestle. After affording his sweetheart and her parents a little sport, William, to bring the matter to a genteel close, began to work himself round with his right leg toward me, as all good wrestlers do; but, seeing that I made no opposition to this principal manoeuvre, he did it in a very careless way, thinking he had to do with a mere novice. Little did he know that this was just what I wanted. He was bringing himself to a position in which it was impossible he could escape me, provided I got the first trip of him, which I took care to take, whipping his right foot in a moment as high as my own knee. This brought him on his back with his full weight, and me above him. The old man uttered three or four exclamations of utter astonishment. 'Thou hess gotten thy backbraid for yince, Willie,' said Miss Armstrong. 'What ailed thee, Willie?' said the wife. 'Thou may weel speer, woman,' said Robie again; 'for, be the saul o' me, I never saw Willie Glendinning sae easily laid on his back aw me lyfe, Ha, ha; Willie, thou jwost fell over as thou had been a corn seck, or a post set up without ony feet.'

'Confound his ignorance!' said Willie; 'whae ever thought of his taking the left foot. It was the cleverest trick I ever saw; but if we twa yoke again!' 'The present time is only ours,' said I, 'If that should chance, you will not find me backward.'

Glendinning seemed loath to give up the right he had so dearly and so nearly won, and tried again and again to get a private word of Jessy, but did not obtain it. He came in, sat down with us, and joined in the general conversation for about an hour; and all the time eyed the lovely heiress so constantly, that I was persuaded he was as deeply in love as I was. Indeed, I never saw her look so comely, or half so elegant, as in her every-day dress. She was in the dress that the country maidens in the Lowlands of Scotland wear; by far the most becoming dress in the world for setting out the female form in all its lightsome ease and elegance, a circumstance well known to our ingenious countryman, David Wilkie. I cannot describe how much more graceful she looked, in her muslin short-gown and demity petticoat, than in her best dress at the fair, and the solemnity at which I first saw her. I see the dress must always bear a proportion to the polish of the mind; and one woman looks most lovely in a dress in which another would look exceedingly awkward.

Among other topics of conversation, they chanced

to fall on one that was not a little irksome to me, and partly explained Jessie's stratagem. 'Does tou ken a chap,' said Robie, 'out amang thy muirs, some gate, that they ca' Geordie Cochrane?' I said I had seen him, but was not intimately acquainted with him. 'He gat his skin tightly threshed at the hiring fair, however,' said he, 'be ane o' our Liddel-head chaps 'at they ca' Tommy Potts. He thought proper to kiss our Jainny, an' gie her her fairing, but he had better hae keepit his kisses and fairings to the sel' o' him, or taen them hame to his muirland lasses an' benty-neckit foresters, for be my certy he gat his dickens.' Here the old bully of a borderer scratched his elbow and his ear, and indulged in a hearty laugh, at the circumstance of Potts having *threshed my skin*, as he called it. Glendinning and the wife joined him, and Miss Armstrong laughed the heartiest of all, seeming to enjoy my predicament mightily.

'Had the fool taen the lassie into a house, out o' sight,' continued old Robie, chuckling, 'he might hae gien her half a score o' kisses, an' then nay man had ony right to pike a hole in his blanket. But, for a stranger to kiss a lass i' the open street, afore a' her sweethearts an' acquaintances, it's bragging them a' to their teeth.' 'We never look on it in any other light,' said Glendinning. 'He needs nae come here,' said Robie, 'an' that ye may tell him, Sandy Welch, frae me; for the man that first gies a hale coontry-side the brag, an then lets sic a chap as Tommy Potts skelp him till he can nouther gang nor stand, sall never cross haffats wi' a bairn o' mine.'

I could not help taking up the cudgels in my own defence; so I said, that I understood my countryman had been provoked beyond sufferance, by vulgar and insulting language; and, moreover, that I had been told there was very little difference in the engagement, by an eye-witness; and that if Cochrane had not been so generous as always to let him up, when he had him under him and at his mercy, the success of the day had been reversed. 'I's unco glad, however, that he gat his hide beasted,' said Robie. 'I likes ay to see a man that brags me coontry come to the woar; and ony chap that wad fling a glass, punch an' aw, in a neighbour's face, deserves aw that Cochrane gat. Be the faith o' me, I never gat sae hard a word frae neay man, but I could hae gien as hard a ane again, rather as be sae belt bursten; he mought hae dung out the chield's herns, an' what wad he hae said for the sel' o' him then? It was a dear kiss to him, Jainny; an' yet thou laughs at it, thou hempy. What's aw this snirtin an' gigglin the night for? I wat weel this is no Geordie Cochrane the sel' o' him?' 'I would not wonder much if it is,' said Glendinning. 'And now I think on't, I could gay my oath it is no other; the ease with which he threw Tommy Potts, and the trip with the left heel.' 'Me, sir!' said I, observing how necessary it was to keep up my lovely maid's stratagem — 'Me! me Geordie Cochrane?' Glendinning was rather damped, and Jessy was like to die with laughing; but as soon as she recovered breath, she said, 'never heed thou what he says, Willie, he's juost Geordie Cochrane — stand to thy point.' 'The devil's in the wench,' thought I, 'what is she about now? Is she first going to lay a scheme, and then blow it up in my face for mere diversion?' I was wrong, and she was right. I believe she took the only method on the emergency; that could have turned them from the right scent. Glendinning looked suspicious; but old Robie, her father, was quite convinced. 'Ah! thou pawky elf,' said he, 'thou's tricking us, and want to set us about the lugs o' ane anowther, to gie thee sport. I'll tell thee what it is, Sandy Welch, thou hast won thysel' a gliff's cracking wi' that skelpie; but an' thou believe aw that she tells thee, thou'lt get few to believe thee.'

With that old Robie began to loose his knee buttons and thrust down his hose, which Glendinning took as a signal, and trudged his way in bad humour, and apparently suspecting, that he left the bonny lass, for whom he had wrestled so manfully, in the possession of the detested Geordie Cochrane. Old Robie conversed with me freely as Sandy Welch, and said, that 'he had heard thae Welches about the head o' Annan war muckle men i' the warld, an' strang i' gear; but, for his part, he likit strength o' beane an sennin better, for that Jainny stwood in nay need o' the ane, but the twother might stand her i' some stead, and might beet a mister meay ways than ane. But wow, man,' continued he, 'they hae durty ill-faurd sheep! I hae seen them stannin i' Staigshawbank, wi' great smashis o' ill-bred tatty things, as black wi' tar as they had been dippit like candle i' the tar kitt; but they had some pith i' their spaulds te.' The idea of bodily strength was always uppermost with Robie; and I conceived, from the thoughtful mood in which he appeared after he had made the last remark, that his mind was dwelling on the idea of the success that the Messrs Welch's black-faced tarry wedders would have had, in wrestling or running, against the Cheviot and mugg wedders of the south. At length, he left us abruptly, and went to bed, with this observation, that, 'if I proved as expert at courting as wrestling, he stood a chance of losing his bit wench.'

Not so indifferent was the mother of the young lady. She appeared dissatisfied, and unwilling to leave her only daughter in the dark with a stranger. She kept poking about the fire with the tongs, and, at every word which was said, either by her daughter or me, she uttered a kind of *hem*, without opening her lips. It sounded to me like a note of pity, mixed with derision, and I did not like the wife at all. She did not, however, venture to expostulate for a good while, seeming afraid of being overheard by her husband; for she was constantly looking over her shoulder toward the bed, in which he had vanished among good woollen blankets, to dream over the feats of his youth in running, wrestling, and putting the stone. Robie's breath began to sound deep — the goodwife's hems became more audible, and by degrees sounded rather like free groans. I wished her a hundred miles distant, and feared that she would mar all my bliss with that lovely and delightful creature, for whom my whole vitals had been so long inflamed with love. 'Gae thee ways to thee bed, mother,' said Jessy, who had till now been working up and down the house. 'What's tou sitting grinning there for; mind I hae been up twae nights this week already.'

'Twae nights already!' exclaimed Mrs Armstrong, alias Mary Park o' the Wolf-cleuch-head, who, having come from the head of Borthwick Water, did not speak with such a full Border accent as either her husband or daughter; 'twae nights already! H'm, h'm! bairn, bairn! I hae aften tauld thee, that sic watchin's an' wakins, an' moopins an' mellins wi' ilka ane, can never come to good. But, d'ye ken, sir, that our Robin's crazed, poor man, about warstling, an' a' sic nonsense. Gude sauf us! I believe he has never thought about aught else a' his days; just as ane could warstle himsel into heaven. O wad he but mind the ae thing needful! an', instead o' gieing our bairn to the best warstler, gie her at night to him that could pray the best prayer.'

'An', be me troth, mwother, I wadna sit five minutes in his company,' said Jessie. 'Does tou ken what Jamie the poyet's sang says? "He that prays is ne'er to trust."* I wad reyther trust mysel' wi' a good warstler, than wi' a good prayer, ony time. I'm quite o' the poyet's mind.'

'H'm! h'm!' said Mary Park, 'sic tree, sic fruit! the thing that's bred i' the bane's ill to drive out o' the flesh. Oh! wow me, what this age is come to! I'll tell thee, Mr Welch, the highest part o' my ambition wad be, to see my lassie married on a minister; ane that wad mind the thing that's good, an' keep by his ain wife an' his ain bed; an' that had a snug house, an' a glibe that he could ca' his ain, an' a round sum ilka year, whatever might happen.'

'I tell thee sae, now,' said Jessie, 'I trow there's mony *ae thing needfu*' wi' thee, mwother. But I ne'er saw it otherwise wi' a religious body yet. A' self! a' self! The very dread o' hell, an' their glibeness o' claughtin at heaven, has something selfish in it. But I'm sure I twold thee, mwother, that I had nae objections to a praying man; the oftener on his knees the better, only let me choice the other. Canst tou pray weel, Sandy? I's sure tou can, for I saw thee turnin' up the white o' thy een at Tommy Rewit's sermon. I'se be bound, aften hast tou had thy neb to a lime wa'.'

'Haud your tongue, ye corky-headit, light-heeled tawpie,' said the displeased Mary Park o' the Wolf-

*From James Hogg's song, 'The Laird o'Lamington,' in his *Border Garland* (1819).

cleuch-head, 'wad ye rin your head against Heaven, an' your back to the barn wa', at the same time? Sorry wad I be to see it; but I'm sair cheatit gin some o' your warstlers dinna warstle you out o' ony bit virtue an' maidenly mense that ye hae, an' fling a' your bonny gowd guineas to the wind, after they hae ye under their thoom. As the tree fa's, there it maun lie; and, as the maid fa's, sae she maun lie too.'

'I ken weel what gate I shall fa', then,' said the implacable Miss Armstrong, who evidently wished, by every means in her power, to put a stop to her mother's religious cant, of which, I suppose, she got many a hearty doze; but it would not do.

'H'm! h'm!' said Mary Park, 'alak, an' wae's me! but what can I expect? If the good seed be sown among thristles, it will spring among thristles; if it's sown in the flesh, it maun grow in the flesh; if it's sawn among stones, it will rise among stones.'

'Hout, fie, mwother,' interrupted the maid; 'thou's no surely hinting that I was sawn in ony o' thae soils? Gin that be Scripture, it's unco hamel made, an' we hae enough ot.'

'Carnality's the mother o' invention,' said the indefatigable mother. 'It is the edder on the hill, that sooks the laverack out o' the lifts. It is the raven i' the wilderness, that cries, flesh, flesh, from evening to morning, an' the mair that ye feed her, the louder is her cry. It is the worm that never dieth, an' the fire that is not quenched. But wo be unto her that thirsteth after the manna of life and the waters of unrighteousness! I send ye to the kirk, an' when I expect ye to come hame like a good heavenly-mindit lass, wi' a' the notes o' the sermon, ye come hame wi' half a dozen profane young hempies at your elbow. I send ye to a' the sacraments round, in hopes that ye'll get a draught o' faith; but a' that ye get is another draught o' sense, an' hame ye come wi' another young man after ye. Your ee's like the edder's, it draws a' the carnal and worldly mindit o' this generation to you; an' sair am I fear'd, that a cast o' grace thou'lt never get.'

'Indeed, but I will mwother, an' thou'lt gae to thee bed, Sandy Welch will gie me ane. He gae me ane already, when he threw Willie Glendinning; for ill wad I hae likit to hae sat another night wi' him. But it was nae cast o' grace for poor Willie. But come, come, Sandy, as I'm sure thou didna come fifty miles to hear a sermon on carnality, I trow thou an' I maun e'en make our bed "low down amang the heather," for a night.'

'Waur an' waur,' said Mary Park, 'wha can take fire i' their bosom an' no be burnt? I hae tried feathers, I hae tried woo; I hae tried a bed o' won hay, an' ane o' fleeing bent; but I fand ay the temptations o' Satan harder on a bed o' green heather than a the lave put thegither. Na, na, an ye will trust yoursel' wi' strangers, keep within your father's door — there's something sacred i' the bigging, an' in the very name. I's e'en gae my ways an' leave ye; my absence will be good company; but, oh! I wish it war *his* will that the days o' warstling an' wooing were ower!' And on saying this, Mary Park, formerly of the Wolfcleuch-head, went groaning to her bed and left us.

I could not help being affected with her words, notwithstanding all the absurdities that she jumbled together. The scriptural style in which her reflections were vented, gave them sometimes a tint of sublimity. I saw that she had fears for her daughter, but wist not well what to fear; and, moreover, that all her ideas were crude and unformed. As for Janet, she was completely her father's child, as the saying is; and actually valued a man principally on his prowess in athletic exercises. No sooner were we left alone, than she lifted my arm, and desired me to hold it up. I obeyed; when, to my astonishment, she clasped her arms round my shoulders and chest, and squeezed me so strait, that I was like to lose my breath. 'This,' thought I, 'is the most amorous girl that ever I met with in my life;' and, judging it incumbent on me to return her caresses, I likewise clasped my arms round her, and was going to lay on two or three sound smacks of kisses on her lips; but she repulsed me sharply, saying, at the same time, 'Thou did'st nae think, fool, that I was gaun to kiss thee; I was only fathoming thy girth round the shoulders. There's no a lover that I hae, but I ken his poust to a hair. Thinks tou I'll sit wi' a lad till aince I ken whither he's worth the sitting wi' or no?'

She next spann'd my wrist, and then, with particular attention, my arm, near the shoulder. 'Thou's no the beane o' our border lads,' said she; 'but there's few o' them better put thegither. I hae nae fund a better shaped, cleaner made arm;' and then she added, with a full sigh, 'I wish thou had but lick'd Tommy Potts.'

I pretended to hold the matter very light, and said, it was a drunken fray, in which no man could answer for the consequences; but I found that nothing would go down — no pretence or excuse was admissible; I must either *lick Tommy Potts*, or give up all pretensions to her. She even let me know, in plain enough terms, that I was a favourite, and that she regretted the circumstance exceedingly; but that indelible blot on my character rendered it impossible for her either to think of me as a lover or a husband. 'What wad my father an' half-brothers say,' said she, 'if I were to marry a man that loot himsel' be threshed by Tommy Potts, a great supple dugon, wi' a back nae stiffer than a willy-wand? It's nae great matter to settle him. He's gayan' good at arms-length, an' a fleeing trip, but when ane comes to close quarters wi' him, he's but a dugon.' I offered to challenge him to fight me with pistols, but that only raised her indignation. She abhorred such mean and cowardly advantages, she said, which was confessing my inferiority in both strength and courage at once, the only two ingredients in a man's character that were of any value. In short, nothing would do, and I was obliged to leave my rural beauty, for whom my heart had been in such pain, without any encouragement. I was, however, greatly amazed with her character; and her personal beauty was such, that I could not help loving her. Her manners were rustic, but not vulgar; and her character, though a perfect anomaly among her sex, was void of affectation. Besides, her fortune was free and unincumbered; no small concern for the son of a poor farmer.

Upon the whole, I thought I could not do less than once more fight Tommy Potts, and either retrieve my lost honour, or die in the skirmish; and with this manful intent, I went to the July fair at Langholm. I soon got my eye upon my antagonist; but who should he be going in close company with, but the identical Willie Glendinning? This was rather an awkward predicament, as I behoved to appear as Sandy Welch to the one, and Geordie Cochrane to the other; so I was obliged to watch them at a distance, and from the way that I saw them looking about, and keeping constantly together, I had no doubt but that they were on some plot against me, either in one of my characters or both.

The day wore to a close, and I saw that they were determined not to separate. I had kept myself sober all the day, that I might have my senses and dexterity in full play; and I was glad to see that Potts seemed to be tippling with great freedom. Resolved not to let the opportunity slip, I got my friend Jock Grieve of Crofthead, a gentleman who feared no man alive, and cared as little either for giving a good threshing, or getting one, as any man I knew of. I took him in, merely on pretence of treating him with a glass before leaving the market, and without apprising him, in the most distant manner, of my intentions of *beginning a rowe*, as it is there called. I knew my mark well; and, in considerable perturbation of mind, led the way into a tent, where sat my two Border antagonists. I chose, as my seat, the form immediately facing theirs, so that when we sat down our noses were almost together. Potts uttered an exclamation of surprise, and instantly held out his hand; but, being determined to stand on no terms with either the one or the other, I refused to shake hands with him. This affronted him greatly; his face grew as red as crimson, and he fell a fretting and growling most furiously. 'Sae thou winna sheake hands wo me, wilt tou nae? Gwod, I rues that I offered. I think I cares as little for thee, as thou does for me, an' I think I has pruven that I needs care as little.' I asked what business he, or any low vulgar rascal like him, had ado to interfere with me; and if it was the custom of this country, that two or three friends could not go into a house, or tent, to talk of business, or enjoy themselves, but they must be interrupted by such beastly jargon as his? 'I chastised you for your temerity in that already,' added I, 'and think you should have taken some care before you ventured to do it again.'

It is impossible to describe his impatience at hearing this. He fidged and grinned, squeezing his teeth together, and doubling his great fists; and at length, with more readiness than any would have thought he was master of, he answered, 'Weal, weal, I's no speak to thee at a'. But tou canna hinder me to speak to my ain neighbour, and tou *sanna* hinder me to speak about what I like. Wullie Glendinning, did'st tou ever hear the like o't, for Geordie Cochrane to say he chasteased me? It is weal known to a' the coontry that I throoshed him till he coodna stand the lane o' him.' 'And sae thou's Geordie Cochrane after a'?' said Glendinning. Jack Grieve, on seeing that ill blood was getting up, thought it was requisite for him, as my friend, to be angry too. 'I beg your pardon, sir,' said he; 'you're in a small mistake; he is commonly calt *Master* Cochrane; and do you call him aught else, at your peril, in my company.' 'And thou's Master Grieve, too, I's uphaud; and I's Master Glendinning; and by Gwod, an' thou ca's me aught else the night, I's won thee a good dadd on the tae side o' thee head.'

It was needless to blow the coal any hotter between these two; there was defiance in every look that past, and in every word that was uttered between them; so that I was left with Potts to renew our quarrel as we chose. I took care it should not be long, having resolved before hand to try his mettle once more. I told him, that the manner in which he had talked of me in the country, I was determined not to bear — that he knew I had it in my power to have finished him two or three times in our first encounter, had I chose — that he should now know his master; and if he had the heart of a flea, he could not refuse to give me satisfaction, after the bragging that he had made. Tommy did not flinch a bit; but accepted of my challenge with perfect readiness, and in three minutes we were hard at it on the top of the Langholm-hill, surrounded by a motley crew of Borderers, of every age and sex. I was perfectly sober; and Potts, though not intoxicated, had drank a good deal. It was certainly owing to this, that I found such a difference in his prowess from the time of our first combat. He fought with violence, but with little caution; and I felt as if he were nothing in my hands. I guarded against every trip, and warded every blow that he aimed with the greatest ease; but his arms were so long and powerful, that my strokes had little or no effect. I never was a good striker, and I could only strike with the right hand. At length, quite conscious of superiority, and perhaps on that account, I made a break at him, and seized him by the shoulder. He made a desperate exertion to free himself, but I seized him by the hair, and the right ear with the other hand, and, in spite of his struggles, closed with him, tripped the feet from him, and gave him a hearty fall. I then gave him two or three sanguine blows upon the temple and left eye, and sprung again to my feet. He was stunned; and as he attempted to rise, I gave him a blow on the shoulder with the sole of my foot, which tumbled him over again, and always as he attempted to get up I repeated it, kicking him in this way down the Langholm-hill before me. He had not as yet yielded; but must have done so in less than two minutes, for he was quite exhausted. At that moment I was knocked down by a side stroke given me by some one, and it was never known by whom. — The Borderers looked on their honour as being at stake in this encounter, and some one had most unwarrantably taken this method of retrieving the day. Jock Grieve blamed Glendinning, who denied it; and these two fought. However, Grieve beat him, and gave him a severe drubbing; but in a subsequent battle with John Glendinning, William's brother, one of the hardest fought that ever was fought, Grieve had rather the worst of it.

I saw nothing of these, having been led, or rather carried into, the tent from whence we issued. For a while I continued insensible, and had no recollection of any thing that had happened; but, after having drank a glass or two of wine, I believed myself recovered. I was grievously mistaken; for the stroke had been given with a staff, or some thick blunt instrument. My skull was slightly fractured, and though the wound did not bleed, it swelled to an unusual size, and grew all discoloured. I was highly indignant at the foul play I had got, and expressed myself in bitter terms against the borderers in general. Indeed, every one, both friend and foe, were alike violent in their execrations of so base and cowardly an assault. But that which provoked me worst of all, was the word that was brought in to me, that Potts had bragged that he gave the blow himself, although at the very moment I was tossing him with my foot. All that I did afterwards, I did very wrong; for it was done in a rage, and whatever is done in that mood is ill done, and repented of. Had I held myself as I was, I had come off honourably enough, and the base conduct of my adversaries would have been universally reprobated; but I abused Potts, and threatened the utmost vengeance on him, as well as on his accomplice who had knocked me down. There were not wanting some to carry this news to Potts, who was soon found, and as ready either to fight me, or shake hands with me as ever; the former of which I imprudently preferred. Alas, the tables were now fairly turned against me, as the stroke on my head had weakened my whole frame. I had no more strength to fight against a waking assailant than a man sleeping and struggling in a dream, and fell an easy prey to Potts. Still I refused to give in, though I could neither return a blow nor ward one; but the onlookers humanely separated us by force.

It was a twelvemonth before I overcame the effects of this blow, being troubled with a swimming in my head, and great debility; but before the expiry of that time, I had quite forgot my Border darling, or thought on her only as a natural curiosity. I was always a favourite with the girls, but never with their parents or guardian. I lost my first love (regretted to this hour) for never having asked her in marriage at any stated period; but grew careless, and so lost her. I am persuaded I lost the next also, for never having asked her for my wife at all; and I lost the third, the loveliest and richest of them all, the beautiful but unconscionable Jessie Armstrong, because I could not *lick Tommy Potts*.

Thus were the days of my youthful passion worn out. They had their delights; but they were not those delights on which recollection loves to dwell; to which the soul turns with serene satisfaction, as the dawnings of future felicity. They were meteors in the paths of folly, gilding the prospects of youth for a season with rays of the warmest and most brilliant hues; but they

dazzled but to deceive, and left the head-long follower
mixed in the pursuits, and obliged to pursue his devious
course in darkness and uncertainty.

From this time forth, I formed no ardent
attachment; I fell into one intrigue after another with
my father's servant girls, and afterwards with my own,
by some of whom I was much plagued, as well as
palpably taken in. But for all those things I had no one
to blame but myself; and, to my shame, I confess, that
in such kind of courses was the prime of my manhood
wasted; and they may say what they will, but every old
bachelor has the same crimes to answer for, in a greater
or less degree. On account of some of my
misdemeanours, I next fell out with the minister and
kirk-session of the parish where I resided, because,
forsooth, I would not submit to do penance publicly in
the church, a foolish and injurious old popish rite,
which I despised and abominated; and this
misunderstanding caused me to lose a lady of fortune a
very few years ago, whom I had courted for
conveniency, and who, for conveniences sake, and, as a
last resource in the world of gallantry, had yielded to
become my blooming bride. And this anecdote, as it is
the last in my love adventures, shall be the last in this
narrative.

I was introduced to this young lady of forty-five at
Edinburgh, on my annual visit to that city, by a relation
of my own. She had been handsome and beautiful, and
she still looked very well, but then she was rouged most
delicately. This I soon discovered, by observing that
her ears and cheeks were of different hues, and I
mentioned it to my relation, who smiled at me, and
said, 'it was better that she should be painted with

rouge than with strong liquors, for when a maid of fashion reached a certain period of life, she must paint either with the one or the other. I acquiesced in this sentiment, though I liked the painting very ill; and, as I conceived it impossible for me to be in a state more unsociable than that in which I was, I paid my addresses to her the more briskly, perhaps because I did not care a farthing whether they were accepted or not. She received my addresses with the greatest politeness, and with a manner truly engaging. I liked her the better, and pushed my suit vehemently, in a correspondence that ensued. Her letters to me were filled with the most beautiful and sublime moral sentiments, with sometimes a dash of affected religious enthusiasm, but not a word of love, save that they always began with the endearing and familiar epithet, 'My dear sir.'

She was a paragon of sanctity and devotion, which I was not fully aware of, as I always suspect very high professions of religion. Her letters contained many hints, that she put the fullest confidence in me; yet, on reviewing all that had past between us, I could not discover when she had ever confided anything to me. They contained allusions to a supposed change of state, between whom it was not mentioned, but no promises. Such circumspection I had never witnessed before.

> Oh! she was perfect, past all parallel —
>   Of any modern female saint's comparison;
> So far above the cunning powers of hell,
>   Her guardian angel had given up his garrison.*

Next summer she came to Moffat, on pretence of

*From Byron's *Don Juan*, Canto I (1819).

drinking the waters; but, in reality, on a reconnoitering expedition to inquire into my character and circumstances. About my fortune she did not care, as she had the means of repairing that; but what she valued as of far greater consequence, the Rev. Mr Johnston and Doctor Singers both spoke well of me. After this my reception was manifestly different, and the cordial shake of the hand, the kind and familiar flirtation, now showed me plainly that the nymph was all my own. I took her hand in mine, and asked her once more to be my wife. 'Oh! Mr Cochrane, you are so cruel! You know that I can refuse you nothing; and you are taking advantage of my weakness, to make me change my pure uncontaminated virgin state for one of care and concern. It is not a light matter for an inexperienced creature like me, to venture on becoming the head of a family, and the mother of a blooming offpsring, whose souls may be required at my hand.' 'Hold!' said I, 'my dear love; that is a secondary consideration, and I don't think that ever they will.' This unlucky expression brought on me a torrent of argumentation, not whether, in the course of nature, my beloved could possibly give birth to a blooming offspring; oh no! such a thought as a negative to that never entered her brain; but whether or not parents were accountable for the sins of their children. She had the Scripture at her fingerends, and gave me, verbatim, Thomas Vincent's Exposition on the Duties of Parents to their Children. Finally, however, she consented to become my bride, from an inward belief, as she plainly acknowledged, that it was the will of Heaven, and fore-ordained to be before the moon or stars were created; and that she might act in conformity with the first and great commandment, 'Be ye fruitful, and multiply, and replenish the earth.'

All this was very well: but, unluckily for me, she came to our parish sacrament, as she went to every one in the bounds. I did not like to see her painted face there. An independent fortune is a snug thing for an old bachelor. On the fastday, when the tokens of admission came to be distributed, I did well enough. I crushed down the stair near the latter end of the crowd, and stood decently in the area, holding my hat in my hand, and waiting as it were my turn. My saintly charmer saw this, and eyed me with looks of heavenly complacency; but when I came opposite to the front door, I slid quietly off, and was never missed. On the Sabbath following, I was not so fortunate when the sacred elements came to be distributed. Until after the first table was served, all went well enough, it having been filled up from the beginning by such of the common people as had not seats of their own. But it was, and is still a custom in our parish, (as absurd a one as can well be) that *the gentry*, as the country people call them, go all into the second table; and there did my charmer go, and there it behoved me to have been also. But there I was not; being obliged, from my disregard of church-discipline, to sit cocking up in the corner of the front gallery all alone. I was not wont to regard this much, as I had some neighbours in the parish, and particularly in the eastern gallery, opposite to me, I could distinctly perceive one in each corner; but I was all by myself, there not being one of the same station near me; and to make the matter worse, the precentor, as he bawled out the following line, looked full at me, — 'Beside thee there is none!'

Sinners are always caught in the net some time or other, which they have themselves prepared. The worst thing of all, my betrothed was so placed at the table, that her eye was fixed on me. She could not lift it but she saw me, and great was the perplexity which that eye manifested. I saw she knew not what to make of it; but, as I suspected, attributed it to the contempt of ordinances. She returned to Moffat in a post-chaise on the Monday evening, and I did not see her till toward the end of the week, when I again visited her. She had not got to the ground of the matter; but, suspecting me of infidelity, she entertained me with a long lecture on the truths of Christianity. I soon convinced her, that I had no doubts to be removed on that subject. 'Why then do you not come forward at the sacrament, like other people?' said she. I never was so sore nonplussed in my life, and could not answer a word. I did not like to tell a lady the plain truth, and had no tale ready to bring myself off — my face grew red, and I had no other shift but to take out my handkerchief on pretence to wipe it. 'Why, me'm,' says I, 'it is excessively warm in this room; do you not think it would be as well to open one of the windows?' 'Certainly, if you wish it, sir,' said she. I opened the window, thrust out my head, and said, 'Bless me! how empty Moffat is at such a delightful season!' 'Mr Cochrane!' exclaimed the lady, 'what is the matter with you? Are you raving? I was talking to you of the bread of life, and the water of life, and asking your objections to the partaking of these; and you answer me, "Bless me, how hot it is! how empty Moffat is!" What does this mean? When the relation in which we stand to one another is considered, I surely have a right to inquire into this most important of all

concerns. Good Lord! if such a thing were to be, as that
I should give up myself to lie in the arms of a castaway
— a child of perdition, to whom it was predestined to
go to hell — and then the iniquity of the father visited
on my children! — I tremble to think of it. Tell me,
then, my dear Mr Cochrane, and tell me truly, what is it
that keeps you back from this ordinance?'

'Why, me'm, really, me'm,' said I —— 'Hem — it is
rather a delicate subject; but, in truth, me'm, it is the
minister and elders who keep me back.' She turned up
her eyes, and spread her hands towards heaven. 'I see it
all! — I perceive it all!' cried she, in holy wrath; 'you are
then an outcast from the visible church — an alien to
the commonwealth of Israel — you are groaning under
scandal, and sins not wiped away; and to ask my hand
while in that state! How could I have set up my face
among my religious acquaintances in town? How could
I ever have looked the reverend and devout David
D—— again in the face, or kneeled at a family
ordinance with the Smiths, the Irvings, or the inspired
H—— G——? And how should I have got my
children, my offspring, initiated into the Christian
church? To have been obliged to take the vows on
myself, and hold up the dear sweet innocents in my own
arms! Oh! the snares, the shame, and the participation
in iniquity, that I have thus providentially escaped —
and all by attending to my religious duties! Let it be a
warning to all such as deride them. Mr Cochrane, either
go and submit to the censures of your mother church,
for your flagrant and gross immoralities, and be again
admitted as one of her members, and a partaker of all
her divine ordinances, or never see my face again.'

'I shall certainly conform to this friendly injunction

for your sake, my dear,' said I; 'though the alternative may be severe, it must nevertheless be complied with. In the mean time, I must bid you a good morning.' Then, bowing most respectfully, I left the room, fully determined which side of the alternative to choose.

From that time forth, I never saw my saintly dame any more; but I got one or two long letters from her, apparently intended to renew our acquaintance, as they were filled up with protestations of esteem, and long sentences about the riches of free grace, which I never read. I had got quite enough of her; for, to say the truth, though I believe it is a fault in me, I have an aversion to those ladies who make extravagant pretensions to religion, and am more afraid of them than any set of reformers in the realm.

Being determined that I would not stand up in my native parish church before a whole congregation, to every one of whom I was personally known, not only to be rebuked, but to hear the most gross and indelicate terms mouthed as applying to my character, and that with an assured gravity of deportment, which makes the scene any thing but impressive, save on the organs of risibility, or the more heart-felt inspirations of loathing. And as my nature could not submit to this, I was obliged to forego the blessings of a devout wife and an independent fortune. Thus it was that I lost my fourth and last mistress; namely, because *I would not mount the stool of repentance.*

Whenever I recounted any of these adventures to my social companions, I remarked that they generally amused them in no ordinary degree. It was this that determined me to make a copy of them, as near to the truth of the circumstances as my memory serves me, and to send them to you, as you are so fond of all narratives that tend to illustrate Scottish manners. I have thought it proper to change two or three of the real names; but the adventures are known to so many in the south west of Scotland, that every individual concerned will be readily recollected; for, saving one gentleman, all the rest, as far as I know, are still alive.

EASTERN APOLOGUES

By James Hogg, the Ettrick Shepherd

The Divinity of Song

As Sadac, the son of Azor, was sitting at the door of his pavilion in the cool of the day, he saw a man approaching, who soon riveted his whole attention. The man was lame, for he had lost a limb; and that limb was replaced by an awkward and unpolished piece of sycamore-wood. When he came nigher, Sadac perceived that he had also lost an arm and one of his eyes; and yet that man, as he came halting along, was singing a strain of so much mirth and gaiety, that he not only appeared to possess a share of happiness, but to be happiness itself personified.

Now Sadac, the son of Azor, was prince of Cathema, and governor over all that country, from the confines of Persia to the great desert of Amerabia; and when he saw this mutilated man of mirth passing by, he called to him to come; but the man regarded him only with a slight glance and a nod, and skipped away over his crutch, singing his song with increased vigour and glee.

Then Sadac called his servants, and said unto them, 'Go, bring that cripple back unto me; for what is he, or what is his father's house, that he should despise the order of Sadac, prince of Cathema?'

And the servants followed the lame man; and the first that overtook him strove to detain him, but he struck the servant of Sadac on the head with his crutch until he fell down, and then the lame man went on singing: and the second and the third came up, and, lo! he did unto them even as he had done to the first; and the men were greatly astonished, and they rose up and returned to their master; and the cripple went on his way, singing as before.

And Sadac was very wroth with the men; and he said, 'Why have ye not detained him and brought him back?' But they answered and said, 'Lo! he struck us on the head and on the hands, and we had no power to stand before him, but fell down as dead men.' And they said, 'Perhaps he is an angel sent from Mahomed;' but Sadac laughed them to scorn.

And he sent out other servants, who were more in number, and mightier than the first; and he said unto them, 'Bring back the man;' and they brought him. And Sadac communed with him, and said unto him, 'Why didst thou not come when I called thee? How daredst thou disobey the command of thy prince and ruler?'

'Because I was then singing to myself a song,' said the lame man; 'and rather than have stopped short in my song, without finishing it, I would that thy head had been struck off and mine to boot.'

And Sadac said, 'Thou shalt surely suffer death for speaking in this manner to the son of Azor, thy prince, and also for lifting up thine hand against the messengers that he sent unto thee.'

And the lame man said, 'If my life will oblige my prince, I shall be exceedingly happy to give it up to him. It is but half a life; for I have given up one half of my body for him and his family already, and the poor remainder is at his service whenever he shall see meet to require it. I will give him up my life, but not my song.'

And Sadac said, 'Was it that wild and foolish strain

which thou wert singing as thou passedst along, and which made thee caper as with ecstasy, and extend thy voice unto strains of happy delirium? Now, by the life of Mahomed! thou shalt sing it before thou stirrest from that spot.'

'Nay, that I shall never do at the behest of mortal man,' said the cripple. 'My prince may take my life, for it is his right; but my song is mine own, and in it he has neither right nor portion.'

And Sadac said, 'How can that be?'

And the lame man said, 'Because it is the child of the soul, and over the soul of man and its lineage thou hast neither power nor dominion. Knowest thou not that the gift of song is an emanation from the Deity? that it is a ray of paradise, enlightening and endowing the immortal part of man with the qualification of angels? that it enriches the soul with a measure of the capabilities of those seraphs who hymn their everlasting hallelujas around the throne of heaven? O thou divine and hallowed gift! what are all the gratifications of sense; what is might or dominion; what are thrones, principalities, and powers, compared with thee, thou sublime intellectual radiance, that connectest man with the hosts above? It was thy holy flame that poured from the mouths of Moses, of David, of Isaiah, and of Mahomed; therefore, hallowed be thy essence, and may no human ruler ever claim dominion over thee!'

And Sadac was greatly astonished, and he gazed upon the lame and mutilated figure as on some superior being; and he thought within himself, 'Why did it not please God and our prophet to endow me, Sadac, the son of Azor, with the gift of song?'

And he said unto the lame man, 'What is thy name?'

And he answered, 'Ismael, the son of Berar, thy servant.' And Sadac said, 'Verily thou art wise as thou hast proved thyself valiant; come within the cover of my tent, and sit thee down here on my left hand, that I may converse with thee about many things:' and the man did as Sadac had commanded him.

The Beauty of Women

And Sadac said unto Ismael, the son of Berar, 'Wherein consists thy great happiness? — for of all the men whom these eyes have ever beheld thou appearest to me to be the most perfectly happy. I have been in search of it all the days of my life — and, oh, how eagerly I have pursued it! — but evermore has it fled from my grasp, and left me the more unhappy on every new enjoyment. So often hath disappointment sickened my soul, that I have resolved again and again to change conditions with the first happy man whom I should meet; and were it possible for me to part with my limb, my arm, and mine eye, I would pleasantly change conditions with poor Ismael, the son of Berar: I would resign to him all my power and all my dominions, with all the riches of Cathema, all my wives, and all my concubines, save one, and with her would I traverse different lands, and try if happiness would follow, for overtaken it will not be.'

And Ismael, the son of Berar, laughed exceedingly, until he even fell backward upon his seat by reason of his laughter, it was so great, and he said, 'O Sadac, thou son of Azor, great art thou in power, and great is accounted thy wisdom, but there is folly with thee, for thou hast been seeking happiness where it is not to be found. But long, long will it be, before the poor son of Berar exchange conditions with thee!'

And he said furthermore: 'After the siege of Bahara, which belonged to Persia, when all the fields and vineyards were laid waste and abandoned, an ox that had been left alive found his way into them; and he gloated over the riches and fertility of the soil, and he consumed, and ate up, and devoured, of all the good and pleasant things, until he was so encumbered with his own fatness that he found it impossible to make his escape from the enclosures; and his soul sickened within him even to loathing, so that he yearned for the liberty of the forest, to browze again on its leaves and dry herbage. But to the forest he could not win, for he was involved in labyrinths of luxury, and the smallest fence could he not surmount, even though but a few feet in height; so that there was he condemned to wallow on in luxury and discontent.

'And the ox observed that every day a wild goat came from the forest which skirted the desert; and the goat was lean and haggard in his appearance, and he skipped lightly over the fences, and browzed greedily on such herbs as he liked for a short space of time; and he would gambol among the flowers, and butt down the young vines and olives as with disdain, and then, bounding over the fences, escape again into the forest.

'And the ox languished exceedingly, and greatly did he envy the goat, whom before he had held in derision; and he watched his approach, and waylaid him, and tried to bring him into conversation, which he at last effected; for the goat fled not from this overgrown victim of luxury.

'And the ox said, "Why liest though not still in these rich pastures and among the vineyards, to feed on all the delicacies of the earth? Why shouldst thou remain so lean, when the fat of the land is before thee?" The goat returned him no answer, but fell a-skipping and dancing round the ox in all the madness of frolic; and he leaped upon the highest walls, vanishing beyond them; so that the ox thought the madcap had gone off to the forest. Then would he appear again, running upon the walls, and bounding over every impediment, until the ox became greatly chagrined; but yet he wished in his heart to change places with that bearded mountebank. Then he called unto him again, and said, "Tell me, I pray thee, why thou wilt not remain amongst these luxuries?" And the goat said, "Because it suits not with my nature and delight to feed myself fat, so as to be coveted for a prey by man, and likewise render myself incapable of escaping from his hand."

'And the ox groaned in spirit, for he perceived that the hint applied to him; and he said, "Lo, I will exchange places with thee; remain thou here, and eat, and drink, and rejoice; and conduct me hence, that I may go into the desert in thy stead." But the wild goat refused, and said, "It lists me not to do so with thee; for were I to remain here I should surely die, and wert thou banished to the desert, after thy feasting and luxury, thou wouldst pine away and die also, even by a death the most tedious and deplorable. Therefore, since thou hast not been able to discern this truth, that a moderate portion of the good things of this life is better than unrestrained luxury and unlimited fulness, in that labyrinth of sloth and sensual gratification must thou remain until thou perish." And while he yet spoke, a band of forayers appeared, and they said one to another, "Behold, what a prey!" And they bent their bows, and took their javelins in their hands, and rushed upon the twain; but the wild goat skipped over the wall, and ere they could let fly their arrows he had bounded away to the forest. But the unwieldy ox became their victim, and fell dead, uttering many grievous and repentant groans, and pierced with a thousand wounds.'

And Sadac, the son of Azor, was grieved in spirit, and his countenance fell, and he hung down his head, and laid his hand upon his breast, and sighed very deeply, and he said, 'Thy story hath made me sad; nevertheless tell me wherein thy great happiness consisteth, and peradventure I may find means of sharing it with thee; for, of all men I ever beheld thou seemest to me to have the least cause of rejoicing, since thou hast lost a limb, an eye, and a hand, and moreover thou art poor, and hast none of the enjoyments of life.'

And Ismael said, 'O my prince, it is because thou hast not learned to discern wherein the enjoyment of life consists. Thou hast not learned, like thy servant, to be pleased with mankind as they are, and with events as they occur; and, when evil befalleth thee, to be thankful that it is not worse. When I lost one of my limbs, fighting in the camp of thy father, I thanked Allah that I had not lost them both. When I lost an eye, fighting in my own cause, I conquered my inveterate enemy, and rejoicing said, "I shall see the clearer with the eye that is left." And when I lost an arm, fighting under thee in the great battle of Bahara, in which the pride of Persia sank before our might, the men who bound up my wound said unto me, "Ismael, thou art sorely wounded and lame besides; retire thou into the tent." But I refused, and said, "I have one hand left, and with it will I fight for my prince until I fall, or the battle be gained." We conquered, and I rejoiced. I know of no man who has more reason to be thankful to God and our prophet than poor Ismael, the son of Berar.'

'I cannot for my life perceive wherein it consists,' said Sadac, 'unless it be in deprivations, which are contrary in their nature to happiness. Tell me one of the chief enjoyments of the heart.'

And Ismael said, 'The highest enjoyment of which my frail nature is capable has been in the endearments of one beloved object — in the society of Abra, my beloved wife, my only spouse, and the darling of my heart. She has proved to me the light of my soul, my crown of rejoicing, my stay and comfort in affliction, and the affectionate sharer in all my joys and sorrows. Ismael, the son of Berar, has had no earthly felicity that can be compared with the love and society of that beautiful, blessed, and divine, creature.'

And Sadac marvelled exceedingly, and he said, 'I have thirty and six wives, and seventy and two concubines, the most beautiful women in the world. They are all pure and without blemish; arrayed in the silken gauze of Cashmere, covered over with jewels and perfumes, and all ready to bestow their smiles and favours on the son of Azor; yet, instead of being my chief joy, from them proceed my greatest earthly plagues and torments. O Ismael, bring thy Abra before me, that I may look upon that beauty which is sufficient to confer such happiness on the possessor.'

But Ismael said, 'Shouldst thou covet and take her from me, thy servant's chief happiness in this world would be extinct.'

But Sadac swore unto him, that though he admired her ever so much, yet would he not deprive him of what he held so dear. 'For I have sufficiency of female beauty already,' added he; 'which when thou seest thou shalt acknowledge.' And he led the lame Ismael away to the apartments of the women, and caused every one of them, amounting to more than a hundred, to pass by before him, and to unveil themselves. They were all beautiful as roses, for they were from beyond the river, and fair of complexion. And Sadac said, 'Thou seest how lovely they are; wouldst thou not exchange thine Abra for any of these?'

And Ismael answered and said, 'No, prince; I would not exchange my Abra for any of these, nor for all, beautiful though they are, which I deny not, though thou shouldst add the wealth of Cathema to boot.'

And Sadac marvelled greatly, and said, 'O Ismael, let me see this wonder of my dominions, whose beauty, single and alone, can ravish and delight a man, and render him completely happy from year to year.' And Ismael did as his prince and ruler commanded, and he brought his wife, and she stood before Sadac the son of Azor. And Sadac said, 'Is this thy wife, even thy beloved Abra?'

And Ismael said, 'It is.'

And Sadac lost all power, and fell from his seat down upon the floor of his pavilion; but it was not with love for the wife of Ismael, but with laughter at the style of her beauty. For the woman was old and homely in the extreme, with a broad brown face, and gray eyes of a heavy and mild lustre. And the servants of Sadac tried to lift him up and to set him on his seat, but they could not, for he had no power either to rise or to support himself thereon; and they said one to another, 'What shall we do for Sadac, the son of Azor, our lord?'

And Sadac laughed seven days and seven nights at the beauty of Abra, the wife of Ismael.

And it came to pass after these days that he called Ismael unto him, and said, 'O Ismael, son of Berar, how hast thou mocked me, by asserting thy happiness with thy Abra, in derision of all the beauty in my harem, collected from the great river Euphrates even to the borders of Media for my pleasure and happiness, which all that beauty has yet failed to produce! But, trust me, Ismael, should we change conditions, thou shalt keep thy Abra for me; for I would as soon think of taking to my embrace the great snake of the desert. If happiness is not to be found with beauty, how is it to be found with woman? Therefore, Ismael, dare not thou any more to mock thy prince.'

And Ismael said, 'Far be it from me to mock my prince, or to tell him any word that is not downright truth. I agree with him, that without beauty there can be no happiness with woman; but of female beauty there are many kinds and degrees; as many as in the whole range of nature besides. There is one beauty of the flowers of the field, another of the storms of heaven, and another of the sun shining in all his glory and strength. So in woman there is one beauty of the skin, and another of the soul; but the one is as superior to the other, as the sun shining in his glory and strength is to the short-lived and fading flowers of the valley. These perish and decay, and fall down in the dust, and are succeeded by others. What striking emblems of the beauty of women, of that beauty of the skin which alone is admired by the son of Azor! But the beauties of virtue, mercy, and benevolence, and all the other glorious qualifications of the soul, have no decay, but continue to advance onward and onward in strength and splendour through time and eternity. Thou, O Sadac, seekest only for selfish gratification, deeming that there happiness is to be found. How certain the event that thou wert to be disappointed! So shall all those be who expect to find true happiness in the pleasures of sense and the vanities of time. But I have sought and found a union of souls that began in youth, has strengthened with age, and will continue to improve and brighten for ever and ever.'

And Sadac went home into his house heavy and concerned, and he said unto himself, 'I would instantly go in search of that union of souls if I wist what it was.'

Maxims of Sadac, the Son of Azor

And Sadac gave unto Ismael a house near to the palace, and a maiden to wait on Abra; and Ismael became a favourite counsellor to his master, who conferred many benefits on him, and conversed with him daily; and the latter days of the old soldier and son of song glided on in happiness. But the nobles of the land envied him exceedingly, and they consulted together and said, 'We must banish this fantastic old man from about our court, else our dignity shall depart from us, and the mean and the vile shall have the dominion.' And one said after this manner, and another after that; but at last it was agreed that out of his own mouth they would condemn him, by reason of the freedom of his expressions. So they forced him into argument, and drove him to wrath by their wrangling, and he uttered words unadvisedly against the divinity of the prophet.

Then they rejoiced in heart, and gnashing with their teeth, as in great wrath, they seized him and carried him before the tribunal of Sadac to receive sentence of death; for there were not wanting abundance of witnesses, who said, 'He hath blasphemed God and his prophet Mahomed.' And Sadac was exceedingly grieved for his friend, for he perceived that there had been a conspiracy against him, and he devised how to save him out of their hands.

And he said unto them, 'O ye nobles and men of Cathema, I perceive the truth of your accusation, and believe that this man's heart is not right as it ought to be with the Lord and with Mahomed his prophet. But, know ye not, O men, and believe ye not, that our holy prophet has all power under God to punish the transgressors of his law and the unbelievers in his doctrine?' And they said, 'We know and believe it.'

Then said he unto them, 'Perceive ye not, also, that our prophet hath vindicated his cause in the eyes of all men? for, lo! hath he not punished this man already for his errors and unbelief as never man was punished before? Hath he not first deprived him of a limb, then of an eye, and latterly of an arm? And since it is so that our supreme prophet hath taken up the vindication of his own cause, it would be unmeet for man to intermeddle between the aggressor and his righteous judge. The cause now lies between them, and let us leave the culprit to the terrible chastisement which the injured Mahomed shall see meet to inflict. I will punish injustice and offences committed against men; but with those committed against God I dare not to interfere. He can punish if he will; but if he sees meet to bear with the offences and contumely of an erring creature, well may I'.

And the men said, 'Our prince hath spoken that which is just and right;' and they went to their houses, and Ismael, the son of Berar, also went unto his house.

And Sadac sent for him afterwards, and said unto him 'O son of Berar, beware how thou again venturest out of thy proper sphere; for as a lamb is among young leopards, or a roe among the cubs of the lion, so is a poor man entering the ranks of the great. Is it not better for thee to be at the head of those of thy own degree — to thrill them with thy songs, to astonish them with thy adventures, and to tell unto them tales that instruct in the beauty of virtue, than to mingle with the nobles of the land, who abhor every excellence in humble life, and among whom thou wilt find thyself like the buffalo among wild oxen, every one having his horn in thy side? Thou art brave in spirit, brilliant in imagination, and intelligent in the virtues of the soul of man; but of the rules of life thou knowest no more than a babe at the breast; yet it is by these that society is directed, and in these can I be thy monitor. Fear thy God, and reverence all his statutes. Honour and obey thy ruler, for a good ruler is the greatest blessing bestowed on a nation; know thy place, and pay deference to all who are above thee in rank and learning, for self-conceit is the mark of Cain stamped on those of low origin. Love all who depend on thee for comfort; do good as far as thou art able; and wish well to the whole human race. These, O Ismael, are the rules of Sadac, the son of Azor; and in the name of the most merciful God and his prophet he strives to observe them.'

And Ismael grew in favour with his prince until the day of his death, and those are his songs that are chanted through all the coasts of Arabia unto this day.

THE FIRST SERMON

By the Ettrick Shepherd

Once, on a lovely day — it was in spring —
I went to hear a splendid young divine
Preach his first sermon. I had known the youth
In a society of far renown,
But liked him not, he held his head so high;
And ever and anon would sneer, and poogh!
And cast his head all to one side, as if
In perfect agony of low contempt
At every thing he heard, however just.
Men like not this, and poets least of all.

　Besides, there are some outward marks of men
One scarcely can approve. His hair was red,
Almost as red as German sealing-wax;
And then so curled — What illustrious curls!
'Twas like a tower of strength! O, what a head
For Combe or Dr Spurzheim to dissect,
After 'twas polled. His shoulders rather narrow,
And pointed like two pins. And then there was
A primming round the mouth, of odious cast,
Bespeaking the proud vacancy within.

　Well, to the Old Grey Friars' Church I went,
And many more with me. The place was crowded!
In came the beadle — then our hero follow'd
With gown blown like a mainsail, flowing on
To right and left alternate. The sleek beaver
Down by his thigh keeping responsive time.
O such a sight of graceful dignity

Never astounded heart of youthful dame;
But I bethought me what a messenger
From the world's pattern of humility!
    The psalm was read with beauteous energy,
And sung. Then pour'd the prayer, from such a face
Of simpering seriousness — it was a quiz —
A mockery of all things deem'd divine.
Some men such faces may have seen among
The Methodists and Quakers — but I never.
The eyes were closely shut — one cheek turn'd up;
The mouth quite long and narrow like a seam,
Holding no fit proportion with the mouths
Which mankind gape with. Then the high curl'd hair
With quiver and with shake, announced supreme
The heart's sincere devotion! Unto whom?
Ask not — It is unfair! Suppose to Heaven,
To the fair maids around the gallery,
Or to the gorgeous idol, Self-conceit.
Glad was my heart at last to hear the word,
That often long'd for and desired word,
Which men yearn for as for the dinner bell,
And now was beauteously pronounced, AY-MAIN!
    Now for the sermon. O ye ruling Powers
Of Poesy Sublime, give me to sing
The splendours of that sermon! The bold *hem!*
The look sublime that beam'd with confidence;
The three wipes with the cambric handkerchief;
The strut — the bob — and the impressive thump
Upon the holy Book! No notes were there.
No, not a scrap — All was intuitive,
Pouring like water from a sacred fountain,
With current unexhausted. Now the lips
Protruded, and the eyebrows lower'd amain,

Like Kean's in dark Othello. — The red hair
Shook like the wither'd juniper in wind.
'Twas grand — o'erpowering! — Such an exhibition
No pen of poet can delineate!

But now, Sir Bard, the sermon? Let us hear
Somewhat of this same grand and promised sermon —
Aha! there comes the rub! 'Twas made of *scraps*,
Sketches from *Nature*, from old Johnson some,
And some from Joseph Addison — John Logan — Blair —
William Shakspeare — Young's Night Thoughts —
                          The Grave —
Gillespie on the Seasons — Even the plain
Bold energy of Andrew Thomson here
Was press'd into the jumble. Plan or system
In it was not — no gleam of mind or aim —
A thing of shreds and patches — yet the blare
Went on for fifteen minutes, haply more.
The *hems!* and *haws!* began to come more close;
Three at a time! The cambric handkerchief
Came greatly in request. The burly head
Gave over tossing. The fine cheek grew red —
Then pale — then blue — then to a heavy crimson!
The beauteous dames around the galleries
Began to look dismay'd; their rosy lips
Wide open'd; and their bosoms heaving so,
You might have ween'd a rolling sea within.
The gruff sagacious elders peered up,
With one eye shut right knowingly, as if
The light oppress'd it — but their features
Shew'd restlessness and deep dissatisfaction.

The preacher set him down — open'd the Bible,
Gave half a dozen *hems!* Arose again,
Then half a dozen more — It would not do!

In every line his countenance bespoke
The loss of recollection; all within
Became a blank — a chaos of confusion,
Producing nought but agony of soul.
His long lip quiver'd, and his shaking hand
Of the trim beaver scarcely could make seizure,
When, stooping, floundering, plaiting at the knees,
He — made his exit. But how I admired
The Scottish audience! There was neither laugh
Nor titter; but a soften'd sorrow
Pourtray'd in every face. As for myself,
I laugh'd till I was sick, went home to dinner,
Drank the poor preacher's health, and laugh'd again.
    But otherwise it fared with him; for he
Went home to his own native kingdom — Fife,
Pass'd to his father's stable — seized a pair
Of strong plough-bridle reins, and hang'd himself.
    And I have oft bethought me it were best,
Since that outrageous scene, for young beginners
To have a sermon, either of their own
Or other man's. If printed, or if written,
It makes small difference — but have it there
At a snug opening of the blessed book
Which any time will open there at will,
And save your credit. While the consciousness
That there it is, will nerve your better part,
And bear you through the ordeal with acclaim.

SEEKING THE HOUDY

By the Ettrick Shepherd

There was a shepherd on the lands of Meggat-dale, who once set out riding with might and main, under cloud of night, for that most important and necessary personage in a remote and mountainous country, called by a different name in every country of the world, excepting perhaps Egypt and England; but by the Highlanders most expressively termed *bean-glhuine*, or *te the toctor*.

The mare that Robin rode was a black one, with a white face like a cow. She had a great big belly, a switch tail, and a back, Robin said, as sharp as a knife; but perhaps this part of the description was rather exaggerated. However, she was laziness itself personified, and the worst thing of all, her foal was closed in at home; for Robin had wiled the mare and foal into the bire with a piece of bread, which he did not give her after all, but put in his pocket in case of farther necessity: he then whipped a hair halter on the mare's head, and the straw sunks on her back, these being the only equipment within his reach; and it having cost Robin a great deal of trouble to get the foal into the bire, he now eyed him with an exulting, and at the same time a malicious, look. 'Ye mischievous rascal,' said he, 'I think I have you now; stand you there an' chack flees till I come back to teach you better manners.'

Robin then hurried out the mare to the side of the kail-yard dike, and calling out to Jean his wife not to be in ower grit a hurry, and to exercise all the patience she was mistress of, he flew on the yaud's back, and off he went at full gallop.

The hair halter that Robin rode with had a wooden snibbelt upon the end of it, as all hair halters had erewhile, when there were no other bridles in Meggat, saving branks and hair halters annexed; consequently with the further end of this halter one could hit an exceeding hard stroke. Indeed, I never saw anything in my life that hurt so sore as a hair halter and wooden snibbelt at the end of it; and I may here mention, as an instance of its efficacy, that there was once a boy at Hartwood mines, near Selkirk, who killed with a snibbelt two Highland soldiers, who came to press his horses in *the forty-five*.

Well, to this halter and snibbelt Robin had trusted for a rod, there being no wood in Meggat-dale, not so much as a tree; and a more unlucky and dangerous goad he could scarcely have possessed, and that the black mare, with a white face like a cow, felt to her experience. Robin galloped by the light of the full moon down by the Butt-haugh and Glengaber-foot about as fast as a good horse walks; still he was galloping, and could make no more of it, although he was every now and then lending the yaud a yerk on the flank with the snibbelt. But when he came to Henderland, to which place the mare was accustomed to go every week to meet the eggler, then Robin and the mare split in their opinions. Robin thought it the most natural and reasonable thing in the world that the mare should push on to the Sandbed, about eight miles further, to bring home the wise woman to his beloved wife's assistance. The mare thought exactly the reverse, being inwardly convinced that the most natural and reasonable path she could take was the one straight home again to her foal; and without any farther ceremony, save giving a few switches with her long illshapen tail, she set herself with all her might to dispute the point with Robin.

Then there was such a battle commenced as never was fought at the foot of Henderland-bank at midnight either before or since. O my beloved and respected editor and readers! I wish I could make you understand the humour of this battle as well as I do. The branks were two sticks hung by a headsteel, which, when one drew the halter hard, nipped the beast's nose most terribly; but when they were all made in one way, and could only turn the beast to the near side. Now the black mare did not, or could not, resist this agency of the branks; she turned round as often as Robin liked, but not one step farther would she proceed on the road to Sandbed. So roundabout and roundabout the two went; and the mare, by a very clever expedient, contrived at every circle to work twice her own length nearer home. Saint Sampson! how Robin did lay on with the halter and snibbelt whenever he got her head round towards the way he wanted her to go! No — round she came again! He cursed her, he flattered her, he reminded her of the precarious state of her mistress, who had so often filled her manger; but all would not do: she thought only of the precarious state of her foal, closed in an old void smearing-house.

Robin at last fell upon a new stratagem, which was this, that as the mare wheeled round whenever her head reached the right point, he hit her a yerk with the wooden snibbelt on the near cheek, to stop that millstone motion of hers. This occasioned some furious plunges, but no advancement the right way, till at length he hit her such a pernicious blow somewhere near about the ear, that he brought her smack to the earth in a moment; and so much was he irritated, that he laid on her when down, and nodding like ane falling asleep. After two or three prolonged groans, she rose again, and, thus candidly admonished, made no further resistance for the present, but moved on apace to the time of the halter and the snibbelt. On reaching a ravine called Capper Cleuch, the mare, coming again in some degree to her senses, perceived that she was not where she ought to have been, at least where it was her interest, and the interest of her foal, that she should have been; and, raising her white face, she uttered a tremendous neigh. The hills to the left are there steep and rocky; and the night being calm and frosty, first one fine echo neighed out of the hill, then another, and then another. 'There are plenty of foals here,' thought the old mare; and neighing again even louder than before, she was again answered in the same way; and, perceiving an old crabbed thorn-tree among the rocks, in the direction whence the echo proceeded, it struck her obtuse head that it was her great lubber of a foal standing on very perilous ground; and off she set at a right angle from the road, or rather a left one, with her utmost speed, braying as she went, while every scream was returned by her shaggy colt with interest. It was in vain that Robin pulled by the hair halter, and smote her on the cheek with the wooden snibbelt: away she ran, through long heath and large stones, with a tremendous and uncultivated rapidity, neighing as she flew. 'Wo! ye jaud! Hap-wo! chywooo!' shouted

Robin; 'Hap-wo! hap-wo! Devil confound the beast, for I'm gone!'

Nothing would stay her velocity till she stabled herself against a rock over which she could not win, and then Robin lost no time in throwing himself from her back. Many and bitter were the epithets he there bestowed on his old mare, and grievous was the lamentation he made for his wife, as endeavouring to lead back the mare from the rocky hill into the miserable track of a road. No; the plague o' one foot would the mare move in that direction! She held out her long nose, with her white muslin face, straight up to heaven, as if contemplating the moon. She weened that her foal was up among the crags, and put on a resolution not to leave him a second time for any man's pleasure. After all, Robin confessed that he had some excuse for her, for the shadow of the old thorn was so like a colt, that he could scarcely reason himself out of the belief that it was one.

Robin was now hardly set indeed, for the mare would not lead a step; and when he came back to her side to leather her with the snibbelt, she only galloped round him and round him, and neighed. 'O plague on you for a beast that ever you were foaled!' exclaimed Robin; 'I shall lose a dearly beloved wife, and perhaps a couple of babies at least, and all owing to your stupidity and obstinacy! I could soon run on foot to the Sandbed, but then I cannot carry the midwife home on my back; and could I once get you there, you would not be long in bringing us both home again. Plague on you for a beast, if I winna knock your brains out!'

Robin now attacked the mare's white face with the snibbelt, yerk for yerk, so potently, that the mare soon grew madly crazed, and came plunging and floundering from the hill at a great rate. Robin thus found out a secret not before known in this country, on which he acted till the day of his death; namely, 'that the best way to make a horse spring forward is to strike it on the face.'

Once more on the path, Robin again mounted, sparing neither the mare nor the halter; while the mare, at every five or six paces, entertained him with a bray so loud, with its accompanying nicker, that every one made the hills ring again.

There is scarcely any thing a man likes worse than this constant neighing of the steed he rides upon, especially by night. It makes him start as from a reverie, and puts his whole frame in commotion. Robin did not like it more than other men. It caused him inadvertently to utter some imprecations on the mare, that he confessed he should not have uttered; but it also caused him to say some short prayers for preservation; and to which of these agencies he owed the following singular adventure he never could divine.

Robin had got only about half a mile farther on his road, when his mare ceased her braying, and all at once stood stone-still, cocking her large ears, and looking exceedingly frightened. 'Oho, madam! what's the matter now?' said Robin; 'is this another stratagem to mar my journey, for all the haste that you see me in? Get on, my fine yaud, get on! There is nothing uncanny there.'

Robin coaxed thus, as well to keep up his own spirits, as to encourage his mare; for the truth is, that his hair began to stand on end with affright. The mare would neither ride, lead, nor drive, one step further;

but there she stood, staring, snuffing the wind, and snorting so loud, that it was frightsome to hear as well as to see her. This was the worst dilemma of all. What was our forlorn shepherd to do now? He averred that the mare *would not* go on either by force or art; but I am greatly deceived, if by this time he durst for his life have gone on, even though the mare could have been induced to proceed. He took the next natural expedient, which was that of shouting out as loud as he could bellow, 'Hilloa! who's there? Be ye devils, be ye witches, or be ye Christian creatures, rise an' shaw yoursels. I say, hilloa! who's there?'

Robin was at this time standing hanging by the mare's hair halter with both his hands, for she was capering and flinging up her white face with such violence, that she sometimes made him bob off the ground; when, behold! at his last call, a being like a woman rose from among some deep heather bushes about twenty yards before him. She was like an elderly female, dressed in a coarse country garb, tall and erect; and there she stood for a space, with her pale face, on which the moon shone full, turned straight towards Robin. He then heard her muttering something to herself; and, with a half-stifled laugh, she stooped down, and lifted something from among the heath, which Robin thought resembled a baby. 'There the gipsy yaud has been murdering that poor bairn!' thought Robin to himself: 'it was nae wonder my auld yaud was frighted! she kens what's what, for as contrarysome as she is. And murderess though the hizzy be, it is out o' my power to pursue her wi' this positive auld hack, for no another foot nearer her will she move.'

Robin never thought but that the mysterious being was to fly from him, or at least go off the road to one side; but in place of that she rolled her baby, or bundle, or whatever it was, deliberately up in a blanket, fastened it between her shoulders, and came straight up to the place where Robin stood hanging by his mare's head. The mare was perfectly mad. She reared, snorted, and whisked her long ill-shaped tail; but Robin held her, for he was a strong young man, and the hair halter must have been proportionably so, else it never could have stood the exercise of that eventful night.

Though I have heard Robin tell the story oftener than once when I was a boy, there was always a confusion here which I never understood. This may be accounted for, in some measure, by supposing that Robin was himself in such perplexity and confusion, that he neither knew well what passed, nor remembered it afterwards. As far as I recollect, the following was the dialogue that passed between the two.

'Wha's this?'

'What need ye speer, goodman? kend fo'k, gin it war daylight.'

'I think I'm a wee bit at a loss. I dinna ken ye.'

'May be no, for ye never saw me afore. An' yet it is a queer thing for a father no to ken his ain daughter.'

'Ay, that wad be a queer thing indeed. But where are you gaun at this time o' the night?'

'Where am I gaun? where but up to the Craigyrigg, to get part o' my ain blithemeat. But where are you riding at sic a rate?'

'Why, I'm just riding my whole might for the houdy: an' that's very true, I hae little need to stand claverin here wi' you.'

'Ha, ha, ha, ha! daddy Robin! It is four hours sin' ye came frae hame, an' ye're no won three miles yet. Why, man, afore ye get to the Sandbed an' hame again, your daughter will be ready for spaining.'

'Daughter! what's a' this about a daughter! Has my dear Jean really a daughter?'

'You may be sure she has, else I could not have been here.'

'An' has she only ane? for, od! ye maun ken wifie that I expectit twa at the fewest. But I dinna understand you. I wish ye may be canny enough, for my white-faced yaud seems to jalouse otherwise.'

'Ye dinna ken me, Robin, but ye will ken me. I am Helen Grieve. I was weel brought up, and married to a respectable farmer's son; but he turned out a villain, and, among other qualifications, was a notorious thief; so that I have been reduced to this that you see, to travel the country with a pack, and lend women a helping-hand in their hour o' need. An', Robin, when you and I meet here again, you may be preparing for another world.'

'I dinna comprehend ye at a', wifie. No; a' that I can do, I canna comprehend ye. But I understand thus far: It seems ye are a houdy, or a meedwife, as the grit fo'ks will ca' you. Now that's the very thing I want at present, for your helping hand may be needfu' yonder. Come on ahint me, and we'll soon be hame.'

I must give the expedition home in Robin's own words.

'Weel, I forces my yaud into the Cleuch-brae, contrary as she was, wi' her white face, for she had learned by this time to take a wee care o' the timmer snibbelt. I was on her back in a jiffey; an', to say truth,

the kerling wi' the pale round face, and the bit lang
bundle on her back, wasna slack; for she was on ahint
me, bundle an' a', ere ever I kend I was on mysel. But,
Gude forgie us! sickan a voyage as we gat! I declare my
yaud gae a snore that gart a' the hills ring, an' the verra
fire flew frae her snirls. Out o' the Cleuch-brae she
sprang, as there hadna been a bane or a joint within her
hide, but her hale carcass made o' steel springs; an' ower
bush, ower breer, ower stock, an' ower stane she flew, I
declare, an' so be it, faster than ever an eagle flew
through the firmament of the heavens.

'I kend then that I had either a witch or a mermaid
on ahint me; but how was I now to get quit o' her? The
hair halter had lost a' power, an' I had no other shift
left, than to fix by instinct on the mane wi' baith hands,
an' cry out to the mare to stop. "Wo ye auld viper o'
the pit! wo, ye beast o' Bashan!" I cries in outer
desperation; but ay the louder I cried, the faster did the
glyde flee. She snored, an' she grained, an' she reirdit
baith ahint an' afore; an' on she dashed, regardless of a'
danger.

'I soon lost sight o' the ground — off gaed my
bonnet, an' away i' the wind — off gaed my plaid, an'
away i' the wind; an' there was I sitting lootching
forret, cleaving the wind like an arrow out of a bow, an'
my een rinning pouring like streams of water from the
south. At length we came to the Birk-bush Linn! and
alangst the very verge of that awsome precipice there
was my dementit beast scouring like a fiery dragon.
"Lord preserve me!" cried I loud out; an' I hadna weel
said the word, till my mare gae a tremendous plunge
ower something, I never kend what it was, and then
down she came on her nose. No rider could stand this

concussion, an' I declare, an' so be it, the meed-wife lost her haud, and ower the precipice she flew head foremost. I just gat ae glisk o' her as she was gaun ower the top o' the birk-bush like a shot stern, an' I heard her gie a waw like a cat; an' that was the last sight I saw o' her.

'I was then hanging by the mane an' the right hough; an', during the moment that my mare took to gather hersel' up, I recovered my seat, but only on the top o' the shoulder, for I couldna win to the right place. The mare flew on as madly as ever; and frae the shoulder I came on to the neck, an' forret, an' forret, piecemeal, till, just as I came to my ain door, I had gotten a grip o' baith the lugs. The foal gae a screed of a nicher; on which the glyde threw up her white face wi' sic a vengeance, that she gart me play at pitch-an'-toss up in the air. The foal nichered, an' the mare nichered, an' out came the kimmers; an' I declare, an' so be it, there was I lying in the gutter senseless, wanting the plaid, an' wanting the bonnet, an' nae meedwife at a'; an' that's the truth, sir, I declare, an' so be it.

'Then they carried me in, an' they washed me, an' they bathed me, an' at last I came to mysel'; an', to be sure, I had gotten a bonny doughter, an' a' things war gaun on *as weel as could be expectit*. "What hae ye made o' your plaid, Robin?" says ane. "Whare's your bonnet, Robin?" says another. 'But, gudeness guide us! what's come o' the houdy, Robin? Whare's the meedwife, Robin?' cried they a' at aince. I trow this question gart me glower as I had seen a ghaist. "Och! huh!" cried the wives, an' held up their hands; "something has happened! something has happened! We see by his looks! — Robin! what has happened? Whare's the meedwife?"

' "Haud your tongue, Janet Reive; an' haud ye your tongue too, Eppie Dickson," says I, "an' dinna speer that question at me again; for the houdy is where the Lord will, an' where my white-faced yaud was pleased to pit her, and that's in the howe o' the Birk-bush Linn. Gin she be a human creature, she's a' dashed to pieces: but an she be nae a human creature she may gang where she like for me; an' that's true, I declare, an' so be it." '

Now it must strike every reader, as it did me at first and for many years afterwards, that this mysterious nocturnal wanderer gave a most confused and unintelligible account of herself. She was Robin's daughter; her name was Helen Grieve; she was married to such and such a man; and had now become a pedlar, and acted occasionally as a midwife: and finally, when they two met there again, it would be time for Robin to be preparing for another state of existence. Now, in the first place, Robin never had a daughter till that very hour and instant when the woman rose out of the heather-bush and accosted him. All the rest appeared to him like a confused dream, of which he had no comprehension, save that he could never again be prevailed on to pass that way alone at night; for he had an impression that at some time or other he should meet with her again.

But by far the most curious part of this story is yet to come, and it shall be related in few words. Robin went with some others, as soon as it was day, to the Birk-bush Linn, but there was neither body nor blood to be seen, nor any appearance of a person having been killed or hurt. Robin's daughter was christened by the name of Helen, after her maternal grandmother, so that her name was actually Helen Grieve: and from the time that Robin first saw his daughter, there never was a day on which some of her looks did not bring the mysterious midwife to his mind. Thus far the story had proceeded when I heard it related; for I lived twelve months in the family, and the girl was then only about seven years of age. But, strange to relate, the midwife's short history of herself has turned out the exact history of this once lovely girl's life; and Robin, a few days before his death, met her at the Kirk Cleuch, with a bundle on her back, and recognized his old friend in every lineament and article of attire. He related this to his wife as a secret, but added, that 'he did not know whether it was his *real* daughter whom he met or not.'

Many are the traditions remaining in the country, relative to the seeking of midwives, or houdies, as they are universally denominated all over the south of Scotland; and strange adventures are related as having happened in these precipitate excursions, which were proverbially certain to happen by night. Indeed it would appear, that there hardly ever was a midwife brought, but some incident occurred indicative of the fate or fortunes of the little forthcoming stranger; but, amongst them all, I have selected this as the most remarkable.

I am exceedingly grieved at the discontinuance of midwifery, that primitive and original calling, in this primitive and original country; for never were there such merry groups in Scotland as the midwives and their kimmers in former days, and never was there such store of capital stories and gossip circulated as on these occasions. But those days are over! and alack, and wo is me! no future old shepherd shall tell another tale of
SEEKING THE HOUDY!

SOME TERRIBLE LETTERS
FROM SCOTLAND

Communicated by the Ettrick Shepherd

DEAR SIR, — As I knew you once, and think you will remember me, — I having wrought on your farm for some months with William Colins that summer that Burke was hanged, — I am going to write you on a great and trying misfortune that has befallen to myself, and hope you will publish it, before you leave London, for the benefit of all those concerned.

You must know that I have served the last three years with Mr. Kemp, miller, of Troughlin; and my post was to drive two carts, sometimes with corn to Dalkeith market, and sometimes with flourmeal to all the bakers in Musselburgh and the towns round about. I did not like this very well; for I often thought to myself, if I should take that terrible Cholera Morbus, what was to become of me, as I had no home to go to, and nobody would let me within their door. This constant fright did me ill, for it gave my constitution a shake: and I noticed, whenever I looked in my little shaving-glass, that my face was grown shilpit and white, and blue about the mouth; and I grew more frightened than ever.

Well, there was one day that I was at Musselburgh with flour; and when I was there the burials were going by me as thick as droves of Highland cattle; and I thought I sometimes felt a saur as if the air had thickened around my face. It is all over with me now, thought I, for I have breathed the Cholera! But when I told this to Davison, the baker's man, he only laughed at me, which was very ungracious and cruel in him; for before I got home I felt myself manifestly affected, and knew not what to do.

When I came into the kitchen, there was none in it but Mary Douglas: she was my sweetheart like, and we had settled to be married. 'Mary, I am not well at all to-night,' said I, 'and I am afraid I am taking that deadly Cholera Morbus.'

'I hope in God that is not the case!' said Mary, letting the tongs fall out of her hand; 'but we are all in the Almighty's hands, and he may do with us as seemeth good in his sight.'

She had not well repeated this sweet, pious submission, before I fell a-retching most terribly, and the pains within were much the same as if you had thrust seven or eight red-hot pokers through my stomach. 'Mary, I am very ill,' said I, 'and I well know Mr. Kemp will not let me abide here.'

'Nay, that he will not,' said she; 'for he has not dared to come in contact with you for weeks past: but, rather than you should be hurried off to an hospital, if you think you could walk to my mother's, I will go with you, and assist you.'

'Alas! I cannot walk a step at present,' said I; 'but the horses are both standing yoked in the carts at the stable-door, as I was unable to loose them.' In a few minutes she had me in a cart, and drove me to her mother's cot, where I was put to bed, and continued very ill. There was never any trouble in this world like it: to be roasted in a fire, or chipped all to pieces with a butcher's knife, is nothing to it. Mary soon had a doctor at me, who bled me terribly, as if I had been a bullock, and gave me great doses of something, which I suppose was laudanum; but neither of them did me any good: I grew worse and worse, and wished heartily that I were dead.

But now the rest of the adjoining cotters rose in a body, and insisted on turning me out. Is it not strange, Sir, that this most horrible of all pestilences should deprive others, not only of natural feeling, but of reason? I could make no resistance although they had flung me over the dunghill, as they threatened to do; but the two women acted with great decision, and dared them to touch me or any one in their house. They needed not have been so frightened; for no one durst have touched me more than if I had been an adder or a snake. Mary, and her mother, old Margaret, did all they could for me: they bathed the pit of my stomach with warm camomile, and rubbed my limbs and hands with hard cloths, shedding many tears over me; but the chillness of death had settled on my limbs and arms, and all the blood in my body had retreated to its conquered citadel; and a little before daylight I died.

For fear of burying me alive, and for fear of any violence being done to my body by the affrighted neighbours, the two women concealed my death; but poor Mary took the sheets, which had been bought for her bridal bed, and made them into dead-clothes for me; and in the afternoon the doctor arrived, and gave charges that I should be coffined and buried without loss of time. At this order Mary wept abundantly, but there was no alternative; for the doctor ordered a coffin to be made with all expedition at the wright's, as he went by, and carried the news through the parish, that poor Andrew, the miller's man, had died of a most malignant Cholera.

The next morning very early, Johnie, the elder, came up with the coffin, his nose plugged with tobacco, and his mouth having a strong smell of whisky; and, in spite of all Mary's entreaties, nailed me in the coffin. Now, Sir, this was quite terrible; for all the while I had a sort of half-consciousness of what was going on, yet had not power to move a muscle of my whole frame. I was certain that my soul had not departed quite away, although my body was seized with this sudden torpor, and refused to act. It was a sort of dream, out of which I was struggling to awake, but could not; and I felt as if a fall on the floor, or a sudden jerk of any kind, would once more set my blood a-flowing, and restore animation. I heard my beloved Mary Douglas weeping and lamenting over me, and expressing a wish that, if it were not for the dreadfulness of the distemper, that she had shared my fate. I felt her putting the robes of death on me, and tying the napkin round my face; and, O, how my spirit longed to embrace and comfort her! I had great hopes that the joiner's hammer would awake me; but he only used it very slightly, and wrought with an inefficient screw-driver: yet I have an impression that if any human eye had then seen me, I should have been shivering; for the dread of being buried alive, and struggling to death in a deep grave below the mould, was awful in the extreme!

The wright was no sooner fairly gone, than Mary unscrewed the lid, and took it half off, letting it lie along the coffin on one side. O, how I wished that she would tumble me out on the floor, or dash a pail of water on me! but she did neither, and there I lay, still a sensitive corpse. I determined, however, to make one desperate effort, before they got me laid into the grave.

But between those who are bound together by the sacred ties of love, there is, I believe, a sort of electrical sympathy, even in a state of insensibility. At the still hour of midnight, as Mary and her mother were sitting reading a chapter of the New Testament, my beloved all at once uttered a piercing shriek, — her mother having fallen down motionless, and apparently lifeless. That heart-rending shriek awakened me from the sleep of death! — I sat up in the coffin, and the lid rattled on the floor. Was there ever such a scene in a cottage at midnight? I think never in this island. Mary shrieked again, and fainted, falling down motionless across her mother's feet. These shrieks, which were hardly earthly, brought in John Brunton and John Sword, who came rushing forward towards the women, to render them some assistance; but when they looked towards the bed, and saw me sitting in my winding-sheet, struggling in the coffin, they simultaneously uttered a howl of distraction and betook them to their heels. Brunton fainted, and fell over the threshold, where he lay groaning till trailed away by his neighbour.

My ancles and knees being tied together with tapes, and my wrists bound to my sides, which you know is the custom here, I could not for a while get them extricated, to remove the napkin from my face, and must have presented a very awful appearance to the two men. Debilitated as I was, I struggled on, and in my efforts overturned the coffin, and, falling down upon the floor, my face struck against the flags, which stunned me, and my nose gushed out blood abundantly. I was still utterly helpless; and when the two women began to recover, there was I lying wallowing and struggling in my bloody sheet. I wonder that my poor Mary did not lose her reason that night; and I am sure she would, had she not received supernatural strength of mind from Heaven. On recovering from her swoon, she ran out, and called at every door and window in the hamlet; but not one would enter the cottage of the plague. Before she got me divested of my stained grave-clothes and put to bed, her mother was writhing in the Cholera, her mild countenance changed into the appearance of withered clay, and her hands and feet as if they had been boiled. It is amazing that the people of London should mock at the fears of their brethren for this terrible and anomalous plague; for though it begins with the hues and horrors of death, it is far more frightful than death itself; and it is impossible for any family or community to be too much on their guard against its baleful influence. Old Margaret died at nine next morning; and what could I think but that I had been her murderer, having brought infection to her homely and healthy dwelling? and the calamity will hang as a weight on my heart for ever. She was put into my coffin, and hurried away to interment; and I had no doubt that she would come alive again below the earth; — but the supposition is too horrible to cherish!

For my part, as far as I can remember, I did not suffer any more pain, but then I felt as if I had been pounded in a mill, — powerless, selfish, and insensible. I could not have remembered aught of the funeral, had it not been that my Mary wept incessantly, and begged of the people that they would suffer the body of her parent to remain in the house for one night; but they would not listen to her, saying that they dared not disobey the general order, and even for her own sake it was necessary the body should be removed.

Our cottage stood in the middle of a long row of labourers' houses, all of the same description; and the day after the funeral of old Margaret, there were three people in the cottage next to ours seized with the distemper, and one of them died. It went through every one of the cottages in that direction, but all those in the other end of the row escaped. On the Monday of the following week my poor Mary fell down in it, having, like myself and her mother, been seized with it in its worst form; and in a little time her visage and proportions were so completely changed, that I could not believe they were those of my beloved. I for a long time foolishly imagined that she was removed from me, and a demon had taken her place; but reason at length resumed her sway and convinced me of my error. There was no one to wait on or assist Mary but me, and I was so feeble that I could not do her justice: I did all that I was able, however; and the doctor gave me hopes that she would recover. She soon grew so ill, and her pangs, writhings, and contortions, became so terrible, that I wished her dead: — yes, I prayed that death would come and release her! but it was from a conviction that she would revive again, and that I should be able to wake her from the sleep of death. I did not conceive my own revival as any thing supernatural, but that which might occur to every one who was suddenly cut off by the plague of Cholera; and I prayed that my dear woman would die. She remained quite sensible; and, taking my hand, she squeezed it and said, 'Do you really wish me dead, Andrew?' I could make no reply; but she continued to hold my hand, and added, 'Then you will not need to wish for it long. O Lord, thy will be done in earth as it is in heaven!'

She repeated this last sentence in a whisper, and spoke no more, for the icy chillness had by this time reached the region of the heart; and she expired as in a drowsy slumber. Having no doubts of her revival I did not give the alarm of her death, but continued my exertions to restore animation. When the doctor arrived he was wroth with me, and laughed me to scorn, ordering the body to be directly laid out by matrons, preparatory for the funeral; and that night he sent two hired nurses for the purpose. They performed their task; but I would in no wise suffer the body to be coffined after what had happened to myself, until I saw the farthest. I watched her night and day, continuing my efforts to the annoyance of my neighbours until the third day, and then they would allow it no longer; but, despite all my entreaties, they took my beloved from me, nailed her in the coffin, and buried her; and now I am deprived of all I loved and valued in this world, and my existence is a burden I cannot bear, as I must always consider myself accessary to the deaths of those two valuable women.

The worst thing of all to suffer is the dreadful apprehension that they would come alive again below the earth, which I cannot get quit of; and though I tried to watch Mary's grave, I was so feeble and far-spent, that I could not but always fall asleep on it. There being funerals coming every day, when the people saw me lying on the grave with my spade beside me, they thought I had gone quite deranged, and, pitying me, they, half by force, took me away; but no one offered me an asylum in his house, for they called me the man that was dead and risen again, and shunned me as a being scarcely of this earth.

Still the thought that Mary would come alive haunts me, — a terror which has probably been engendered within me by the circumstances attending my own singular resuscitation. And even so late as the second night after her decease, as I was watching over her with prayers and tears, I heard a slight gurgling in her throat, as if she had been going to speak: there was also, I thought, a movement about the breast, and one of the veins of the neck started three or four times. How my heart leaped for joy as I breathed my warm breath into her cold lips! but movement there was no more. And now, Sir, if you publish this letter, let it be with an admonition for people to be on their guard when their friends are suddenly cut off by this most frightful of all diseases, for it is no joke to be buried alive.

I have likewise heard it stated, that one boy fell a-kicking the coffin on his way to the grave, who is still living and life-like, and that a girl, as the doctors were cutting her up, threw herself off the table. I cannot vouch for the truth of these singular and cruel incidents, although I heard them related as facts; but with regard to my own case there can be no dispute.

It does a great deal of ill to the constitution to be too frightened for this scourge of God; but temerity is madness, and caution prudence: for this may be depended on, that it is as infectious as fire. But then, when fire is set to the mountain, it is only such parts of its surface as are covered with decayed garbage that is combustible, while over the green and healthy parts of the mountain the flame has no power; and any other reasoning than this is worse than insanity.

For my part, I have been very hardly used, there having been few harder cases than my own. In Lothian every one shunned me; and the constables stopped me on the road, and would not even suffer me to leave the county, — the terror of infection is so great. So dreadful are the impressions of fear on some minds, that it has caused a number of people both in Scotland and England to hang themselves, or otherwise deprive themselves of life, as the only sure way of escaping its agonies.

Finding myself without a home and without employment, I made my escape over the tops of the Lammermuirs, keeping out of sight of any public road, and by that means escaped into Teviotdale, where I changed my name to Ker, and am now working at day-labour in the town of Roxburgh, and on the farms around; and though my name was Clapperton when I wrought with you, I must now sign myself your humble servant,

ANDREW KER.

[The next is in some degree different, though likewise narrating very grievous circumstances. It is written by the mate of The Jane Hamilton of Port Glasgow.]

SIR, — I now sit down to give you the dismal account of the arrival of the Cholera in the west of Scotland. I sent it a month ago to a friend in London, to put into the newspapers, but it never appeared; so if you think it worth while, you may publish it. But if there be any paper or periodical that Campbell or Galt* is connected with, I would rather it were sent to one of them, as they

*The Scottish poet Thomas Campbell and novelist John Galt both lived in London, and were acquaintances of James Hogg.

are both acquaintances and old schoolfellows, and will remember me very well.

Well then, Sir, you must know that in our passage from Riga to Liverpool, in January, we were attacked by very squally weather off the western coast of Scotland, and were obliged to put into one of those interminable narrow bays denominated lochs, in Argyleshire, where we cast anchor on very bad ground.

I cannot aver that our ship was perfectly clean, for we lost one fine old fellow by the way, and several others were very bad; so I was sent off to a mining or fishing village, to procure some medicine and fresh meat. Our captain had an immensely large black Newfoundland dog, whose name was Oakum, and who always attached himself to me, and followed me; but that day he chanced not to go ashore with me. Some time afterwards, some of the sailors going on shore to play themselves, Oakum went with them, and coming on the scent of my track he followed it. Now the natives had some way heard that the Cholera was come with the ship; but so little did they conceive what it was, that they were nothing afraid of coming in contact with me.

The village grocer, draper, hatter, and apothecary, had no medicines on hand, save Glauber's salts, and of these he had two corn-sacks full. I bought some; and while I was standing and bargaining about the price of a pig, I beheld a terrible commotion in the village: the men were stripped, and running as for a race; and the women were screaming and running after them, some of them having a child on their backs, and one below each arm, while the Gaelic was poured and shouted from every tongue. 'What is it? What in the world is it?' said I to the merchant, who had a little broken English. 'Oh,

she pe tat tam bhaist te Collara Mòr,' said he; and away
he ran with the rest.

It so happened that one Donald M'Coll was going
down the coast on some errand, and meeting with
Oakum with his broad gilded collar about his neck, he
instantly knew who he was; and, alarmed beyond
expression, he took to his heels, threw off his coat and
bonnet and ran, giving the alarm all the way as he went;
and men, women, and children, betook them to flight
into the recesses of the mountains, where they lay
peeping over the rocks and the heath, watching the
progress of this destroying angel.

Honest Oakum was all the while chopping out of one
cottage into another, enjoying the scraps exceedingly,
which the people had left behind them in their haste.
Yea, so well satisfied was he with his adventure, that he
did not return until after dark, so that the Highlanders
did not know he had returned at all. The people had not
returned to their houses when we came away.

But the most singular circumstance is yet to relate.
On our return to the Clyde from Liverpool, where we
rode quarantine, we learnt that the Cholera Morbus had
actually broken out in that village, — at least a most
inveterate diarrhoea, accompanied with excessive pains
and vomiting, which carried off a number of the
inhabitants; but, the glen being greatly overstocked,
they were not much missed. Such a thing as Cholera
Morbus or sending for a doctor never entered their
heads, but a terrible consumption of the merchant's
Glauber's salts ensued; and when no more could be
done for their friends, they buried them, and then there
was no more about it. Whether the disease was
communicated to them by the dog, by myself, by the

fright, or the heat they got in running, I cannot determine; but it is certain the place suffered severely. They themselves alleged as the cause, their having 'peen raiter, and te raiter too heafy on te herring and pot-hato.' It was from thence that the disease was communicated to Kirkintilloch by a single individual. Oakum continues in perfect health; but was obliged to undergo fumigation and a bath, by way of quarantine, which he took highly amiss.

I am, Sir, your obedient servant,
ALEXANDER M'ALISTER.

[The next is the most hideous letter of all. We wish the writer may be quite in his right mind. But save in a little improvement in the orthography and grammar, we shall give it in his own words.]

SIR, — Although I sent the following narrative to an Edinburgh newspaper, with the editor of which I was well acquainted; yet he refused to give it publicity, on the ground that it was only a dream of the imagination: but if a man cannot be believed in what he hears and sees, what is he to be believed in? Therefore, as I am told that you have great influence with the printers in London, I will thank you to get this printed; and if you can get me a trifle for it, so much the better.

I am a poor journeyman tradesman in the town of Fisherrow, and I always boarded with my mother and two sisters, who were all in the trade;[1] but my mother was rather fond of gossiping and visiting, and liked to get a dram now and then. So when that awful plague of

[1] Probably the fish trade

Cholera came on us for the punishment of our sins, my mother would be running to every one that was affected; and people were very glad of her assistance, and would be giving her drams and little presents; and for all that my sisters and I could say to her, she would not be hindered.

'Mother,' said I to her, one night, 'gin ye winna leave aff rinning to infectit houses this gate, I'll be obliged to gang away an' leave ye an' shift for mysel' some gate else; an' my sisters shall gang away an' leave ye too. Do ye no consider, that ye are exposing the whole o' your family to the most terrible of deaths; an' if ye should bring infection among us, an' lose us a', how will ye answer to God for it?'

'Hout, Jamie, my man, ye make aye sic a wark about naething!' quoth she; 'I am sure ye ken an' believe that we are a' in our Maker's hand, and that he can defend us frae destruction that walketh at noonday, and from the pestilence that stealeth in by night?'

'I allow that, mother,' quoth I; 'I dinna misbelieve in an overruling Providence. But in the present instance, you are taking up an adder, and trusting in Providence that the serpent winna sting you and yours to death.'

'Tush! Away wi' your grand similitudes, Jamie,' said she; 'ye were aye ower-learned for me. I'll tell ye what I believe. It is, that if we be to take the disease an' dee in it, we'll take the disease an' dee in it; and if it is otherwise ordained, we'll neither take it nor dee in it: for my part, I ken fu' weel that I'll no be smittit, for the wee drap drink, whilk ye ken I always take in great moderation, will keep me frae taking the infection; an' if ye keep yoursels a' tight an' clean, as ye hae done, the angel o' Egypt will still pass by your door an' hurt you not.'

'I wot weel,' said my sister Jane, 'I expect every day to be my last, for my mither will take nae body's advice but her ain. An' weel do I ken that if I take it I'll dee in it. I hae the awfu'est dreams about it! I dreamed the last night that I dee'd o' the plague, an' I thought I set my head out o' the cauld grave at midnight, an' saw the ghosts of a' the Cholera fok gaun trailing about the kirk-yard wi' their white withered faces an' their glazed een; an' I thought I crap out o' my grave an' took away my mother and brother to see them, an' I had some kind o' impression that I left Annie there behind me.'

'O! for mercy's sake, haud your tongue, lassie,' cried Annie; 'I declare ye gar a' my flesh creep to hear you. It is nae that I'm ony feard for death in ony other way but that. But the fearsome an' loathsome sufferings, an' the fearsome looks gars a' ane's heart grue to think o'. An' yet our mither rins the hale day frae ane to anither, and seems to take a pleasure in witnessing their cries, their writhings, and contortions. I wonder what kind o' heart she has, but it fears me it canna be a right ane.'

My poor dear sister Annie! she fell down in the Cholera the next day, and was a corpse before midnight; and, three days after, her sister followed her to the kirk-yard, where their new graves rise side by side thegither among many more. To describe their sufferings is out of my power, for the thoughts of them turns me giddy, so that I lose the power of measuring time, sometimes feeling as if I had lost my sisters only as it were yesterday, and sometimes an age ago. From the moment that Annie was seized, my state of mind has been deplorable; I expected every hour to fall a victim to it myself: but as for my mother, she bustled about as if it had been some great event in which it behoved her to make an imposing figure. She scolded the surgeon, the officers of the Board of Health, and even the poor dying girls, for their unearthly looks and cries. 'Ye hae muckle to cry for,' cried she; 'afore ye come through what I hae done in life, ye'll hae mair to cry for nor a bit cramp i' the stomach.'

When they both died she was rather taken short, and expressed herself as if she weened that she had not been fairly dealt with by Providence, considering how much she had done for others; but she had that sort of nature in her that nothing could daunt or dismay, and continued her course — running to visit every Cholera patient within her reach, and going out and coming in at all times of the night.

After nine or ten days, there was one Sabbath night that I was awoke by voices which I thought I knew; and on looking over the bed, I saw my two sisters sitting one on each side of my mother, conversing with her, while she was looking fearfully first to the one and then to the other; but I did not understand their language, for they seemed to be talking keenly of a dance.

My sisters having both been buried in their Sunday clothes, and the rest burnt, the only impression I had was, that they had actually come alive and risen from the grave; and if I had not been naked at the time I would have flown to embrace them, for there were reports of that kind going. But when I began to speak, Jane held up her hand and shook her head at me; and I held my peace, for there was a chilness and terror came over me; yet it was not for my sisters, for they had no appearance of being ghosts: on the contrary, I thought I never saw them look so beautiful. They continued talking of their dance with apparent fervour; and I heard one of them saying, it was a dance of death, and held in the churchyard. And as the plague of Cholera was a breath of hell, they who died of it got no rest in their graves, so that it behoved all, but parents in particular, to keep out of its influences till the vapour of death passed over.

'But now, dear mother, you must go with us and see,' said Annie.

'Oh, by all means!' said Jane, 'since you have introduced us into such splendid company, you must go with us, and see how we act our parts.' 'Come along, come along.' cried both of them at the same time; and they led my mother off between them: she never spoke, but continued to fix the most hideous looks first on the one and then on the other. She was apparently under the power of some supernatural influence, for she manifested no power of resistance, but walked peaceably away between them. I cried with a tremulous voice, 'Dear, dear sisters, will you not take me with you too?' But Annie, who was next me, said, 'No, dearest brother, lie still and sleep till your Redeemer wakes you — We will come for you again.'

I then felt the house fall a-wheeling round with me, swifter than a mill-wheel, the bed sank, and I fell I knew not whither. The truth is, that I had fainted, for I remember no more until next day. As I did not go to work at my usual time, my master had sent his 'prentice-boy to inquire about me, thinking I had been attacked by Cholera. He found me insensible, lying bathed in cold sweat, and sent some of the official people to me, who soon brought me to myself. I said nothing of what I had seen; but went straight to the churchyard, persuaded that I would find my sisters' graves open, and they out of them; but, behold! they were the same as I left them, and I have never seen mother or sisters more. I could almost have persuaded myself that I had been in a dream, had it not been for the loss of my mother; but as she has not been seen or heard of since that night, I must believe all that I saw to have been real. I know it is suspected both here and in Edinburgh, that she has been burked, as she was always running about by night; but I know what I saw, and must believe in it though I cannot comprehend it.

Yours most humbly,
JAMES M'L——.

SCOTTISH HAYMAKERS

By the Ettrick Shepherd

There is no employment in Scotland so sweet as working in a hay-field on a fine summer day. Indeed it is only on a fine summer day that the youths and maidens of this northern clime can work at the hay. But then the scent of the new hay, which of all others in the world is the most delicious and healthful, the handsome dress of the girls, which is uniformly the same, consisting of a snow-white bedgown and white or red striped petticoat, the dress that Wilkie is so fond of, and certainly the most lovely and becoming dress that ever was or ever will be worn by woman; and then the rosy flush of healthful exercise on the cheeks of the maidens, with their merry jibes and smiles of innocent delight! Well do I know, from long and well tried experience, that it is impossible for any man with the true feelings of a man to work with them or even to stand and look on — both of which I have done a thousand times, first as a servant, and afterwards as a master — I say it is impossible to be among them and not to be in love with some one or other of them.

But this simple prologue was merely meant to introduce a singular adventure I met with a good many years ago. Mr Terry, the player, his father and brother-in-law, the two celebrated Naesmiths, and some others, among whom was Monsieur Alexandre, the most wonderful ventriloquist that I believe ever was born, and I think Grieve and Scott, but at this distance of time I am uncertain, were of the party. However, we met by appointment; and, as the weather was remarkably fine, agreed to take a walk into the country and dine at 'The Hunter's Tryste,' a little, neat, cleanly, well-kept inn, about two miles to the southward of Edinburgh. We left the city by the hills of Braid, and there went into a hay-field. The scene certainly was quite delightful, what with the scent of the hay, the beauty of the day, and the rural group of haymakers. Some were working hard, some wooing, and some towzling as we call it, when Alexander Naesmith, who was always on the look-out for any striking scene of nature, called to his son — 'Come here, Peter, and look at this scene. Did you ever see aught equal to this? Look at those happy haymakers on the foreground; that fine old ash tree and the castle between us and the clear blue sky. I declare I have hardly ever seen such a landscape! And if you had not been a perfect stump as you are, you would have noticed it before me. If you had I would have set ten times more value on it.'

'Oh! I saw it well enough,' said Peter, 'and have been taking a peep at it this while past, but I hae some other thing to think of and look at just now. Do you see that girl standing there with the hay-rake in her hand?'

'Ay now, Peter, that's some sense,' said the veteran artist. 'I excuse you for not looking at the scene I was sketching. Do you know, man, that is the only sensible speech I ever heard you make in my life.'

There were three men and a very handsome girl loading an immense cart of hay. We walked on, and at length this moving hay-stack overtook us. I remember it well, with a black horse in the shafts and a fine light grey one in the traces. We made very slow progress; for Naesmith would never cease either sketching or stopping us to admire the scenery of nature, and I remember he made a remark to me that day which I think neither he nor his most ingenious son, now no more, ever attended much to; for they have often drawn most extensive vistas the truest to nature of any thing I ever saw in my uncultivated judgment, which can only discern what is accordant with nature by looking on nature itself: but, if a hundred years hence the pictures of the Naesmiths are not held invaluable, I am no judge of true natural scenery. But I have forgot myself. The remark that he made to me was this: 'It is amazing how little makes a good picture; and frequently the less that is taken in the better.' Some of the ladies of the family seem to have improved greatly on this hint.

But to return to my story. We made such slow progress on account of Naesmith, that up came the great cart-load of hay on one side of us, with a great burly Lothian peasant sitting upon the hay, lashing on his team, and whistling his tune. We walked on, side by side, for a while, I think about half a mile, when, all at once, a child began to cry in the middle of the cart-load of hay. I declare I was cheated myself; for, though I was walking alongside of Alexandre, I thought there was a child among the hay; for it cried with a kind of half smothered breath, that I am sure there never was such a deception practised in this world. Peter Naesmith was leaning on the cart-shaft at the time, and conversing with the driver about the beautiful girl he had seen in the hay-field. But Peter was rather deaf, and, not hearing the screaming of the child, looked up in astonishment, when the driver of the cart began to stare around him like a man bereaved of his senses.

'What is the meaning of this?' said Terry. 'You are smothering a child among your hay.'

The poor fellow, rough and burly as was his outer man, was so much appalled at the idea of taking infant life, that he exclaimed in a half-articulate voice: 'I wonder how they could fork a bairn up to me frae the meadow, an' me never ken!' And without taking time to descend to loose his cart-ropes, he cut them through the middle, and turned off his hay, roll after roll, with the utmost expedition; and still the child kept crying almost under his hands and feet. He was even obliged to set his feet on each side of the cart for fear of trampling the poor infant to death. At length, when he had turned the greater part of the hay off upon the road, the child fell a-crying most bitterly amongst the hay, on which the poor fellow, (his name was Sandy Burnet), jumped off the cart in the greatest trepidation. 'Od! I hae thrawn the poor thing ower!' exclaimed he. 'I's warrant it's killed' — and he began to shake out the hay with the greatest caution. I and one of my companions went forward to assist him. 'Stand back! stand back!' cried he. 'Ye'll maybe tramp its life out. I'll look for't mysel'.' But, after he had shaken out the whole of the hay, no child was to be found. I never saw looks of such amazement as Sandy Burnet's then were. He seemed to have lost all comprehension of every thing in this world. I was obliged myself to go on to the brow of the hill and call on some of the haymakers to come and load the cart again.

Mr Scott and I stripped off our coats, and assisted; and, as we were busy loading the cart, I said to Sandy, seeing him always turning the hay over and over for fear of running the fork through a child, 'What can hae become o' the creature, Sandy? — for you must be sensible that there was a bairn among this hay.'

'The Lord kens, sir,' said Sandy.

'Think ye the lasses are a' safe enough an' to be trusted?' said I.

'For ony thing that I ken, sir.'

'Then where could the bairn come frae?'

'The Lord kens, sir. That there was a bairn, or the semblance o' ane, naebody can doubt; but I'm thinking it was a fairy, an' that I'm hauntit.'

'Did you ever murder any bairns, Sandy?'

'Oh no! I wadna murder a bairn for the hale world.'

'But were ye ever the cause o' any lasses murdering their bairns?'

'Not that I ken o'.'

'Then where could the bairn come frae? — for you are sensible that there is or was a bairn amang your hay. It is rather a bad-looking job, Sandy, and I wish you were quit of it.'

'I wish the same, sir. But there can be nae doubt that the creature among the hay was either a fairy or the ghaist of a bairn, for the hay was a' forkit off the swathe on the meadow. An' how could ony body fork up a bairn, an' neither him nor me ken?'

We got the cart loaded once more, knitted the ropes firmly, and set out; but we had not proceeded a hundred yards before the child fell a-crying again among the hay with more vehemence and with more choaking screams than ever. 'Gudeness have a care o' us! Heard ever ony leevin the like o' that! I declare the creature's there again!' cried Sandy, and, flinging himself from the cart with a summerset, he ran off, and never once looked over his shoulder as long as he was in our sight. We were very sorry to hear afterwards that he fled all the way to the highlands of Perthshire, where he still lives in a deranged state of mind.

We dined at 'The Hunter's Tryste,' and spent the afternoon in hilarity; but such a night of fun as Monsieur Alexandre made us I never witnessed and never shall again. On the stage, where I had often seen him, his powers were extraordinary, and altogether unequalled; that was allowed by every one: but the effect there was not to be compared with that which he produced in a private party. The family at the inn consisted of the landlord, his wife, and her daughter, who was the landlord's step-daughter, a very pretty girl, and dressed like a lady; but, I am sure that family never spent an afternoon of such astonishment and terror from the day they were united until death parted them — though they may be all living yet, for any thing that I know, for I have never been there since. But Alexandre made people of all ages and sexes speak from every part of the house, from under the beds, from the basin-stands, and from the garret, where a dreadful quarrel took place. And then he placed a bottle on the top of the clock, and made a child scream out of it, and declare that the mistress had corked it in there to murder it. The young lady ran, opened the bottle, and looked into it, and then, losing all power with amazement, she let it fall from her hand and smashed it to pieces. He made a bee buz round my head and face until I struck at it several times and had nearly felled myself. Then there was a drunken man came to the door, and insisted in a rough obstreperous manner on being let in to shoot Mr Hogg; on which the landlord ran to the door and bolted it, and ordered the man to go about his business for there was no room in the house, and there he should not enter on any account. We all heard the voice of the man going round and round the house, grumbling, swearing, and threatening, and all the while Alexandre was just standing with his back to us at the room-door, always holding his hand to his mouth, but nothing else. The people ran to the windows to see the drunken man going by, and Miss Jane even ventured to the corner of the house to look after him; but neither drunken man nor any other man was to be seen. At length, on calling her in to serve us with some wine and toddy, we heard the drunken man's voice coming in at the top of the chimney. Such a state of amazement as Jane was in I never beheld. 'But ye neednae be feared, gentlemen,' said she, 'for I'll defy him to win down. The door's boltit an' lockit, an' the vent o' the lumb is na sae wide as that jug.'

However, down he came, and down he came, until his voice actually seemed to be coming out of the grate. Jane ran for it, saying, 'He is winning down, I believe, after a'. He is surely the deil!'

Alexandre went to the chimney, and, in his own natural voice ordered the fellow to go about his business, for into our party he should not be admitted, and if he forced himself in he would shoot him through the heart. The voice then went again grumbling and swearing up the chimney. We actually heard him hurling down over the slates, and afterwards his voice dying away in the distance as he vanished into Mr Trotter's plantations. We drank freely, and paid liberally, that afternoon; but I am sure the family never were so glad to get quit of a party in all their lives.

To prove the authenticity of this story, I may just mention that Peter Naesmith and Alexander ran a race in going home for half a dozen of wine, and, it being down hill, Peter fell and hurt his breast very badly. I have been told that that fall ultimately occasioned his death. I hope it was not so; for, though a perfect simpleton, he was a great man in his art.

Suggestions for Further Reading

Some Books by James Hogg:

Anecdotes of Sir W. Scott, ed. Douglas S. Mack. Edinburgh: Scottish Academic Press, 1983.

The Brownie of Bodsbeck, ed. Douglas S. Mack. Edinburgh: Scottish Academic Press, 1976.

James Hogg: Selected Stories and Sketches, ed. Douglas S. Mack. Edinburgh: Scottish Academic Press, 1982.

Memoir of the Author's Life and *Familiar Anecdotes of Sir Walter Scott*, ed. Douglas S. Mack. Edinburgh: Scottish Academic Press, 1972.

The Private Memoirs and Confessions of a Justified Sinner, ed. John Carey. London: Oxford University Press, 1969.

The Private Memoirs and Confessions of a Justified Sinner, ed. John Wain. Middlesex: Penguin, 1983.

The Three Perils of Man: War, Women and Witchcraft, ed. Douglas Gifford. Edinburgh: Scottish Academic Press, 1972.

Some Recent Studies:

Ian Campbell, 'Hogg's *Confessions* and the *Heart of Darkness*,' *Studies in Scottish Literature*, XV (1980), 187-201.

David Eggenschwiler, 'James Hogg's *Confessions* and the Fall Into Division,' *Studies in Scottish Literature*, July 1972, pp. 26-39.

David Groves, 'James Hogg's *Confessions* and the Vale of Soul-Making,' *Studies in Scottish Fiction: The Nineteenth Century*, ed. Horst W. Drescher. Mainz, Germany, forthcoming.

——, 'James Hogg's "Singular Dream" and the *Confessions*,' *Scottish Literary Journal*, May 1983, pp. 54-66.

——, 'Myth and Structure in James Hogg's *Three Perils of Woman*,' *Wordsworth Circle*, Autumn 1982, pp. 203-210.

Douglas Mack, 'Hogg's Religion and *The Confessions of a Justified Sinner*,' *Studies in Scottish Literature*, April 1970, pp. 272–75.

The Newsletter of the James Hogg Society, ed. Gillian H. Hughes. Stirling University, 1982–

Norah Parr, *James Hogg at Home: Being the Domestic Life and Letters of the Ettrick Shepherd*. Dollar: Douglas S. Mack, 1980.

Scottish Literary Journal, May 1983 (special James Hogg number), ed. Thomas Crawford.

Notes to the Introduction

1 Byron, letter to John Murray, 12 Oct., 1820, reprinted in *Byron's Letters and Journals*, 12 vols., ed. Leslie A. Marchand (London, 1973-82), VII, 200.

2 James Hogg, 'Memoir of the Author's Life,' in *James Hogg: MEMOIR OF THE AUTHOR'S LIFE and FAMILIAR ANECDOTES OF SIR WALTER SCOTT*, ed. Douglas S. Mack (Edinburgh and London, 1972), pp. 7, 10-11, 11.

3 James Hogg, *A Series of Lay Sermons on Good Principles and Good Breeding* (London, 1834), p. 274.

4 This interpretation is developed in my article, 'Parallel Narratives in James Hogg's *Justified Sinner*,' *Scottish Literary Journal*, Dec. 1982, pp. 57-63.

5 Hogg, *Lay Sermons*, pp. 281, 276.

6 James Hogg, letter to Archibald Constable, 20 May, 1813, reprinted in Thomas Constable, *Archibald Constable and his Literary Correspondents*, 3 vols. (London, 1873), II, 36.

7 Hogg, *Lay Sermons*, p. 276.

8 Hogg, 'Memoir of the Author's Life,' p. 18.

9 [Dr James Browne], *The 'Life' of the Ettrick Shepherd Anatomized; in a Series of Strictures on the Autobiography of James Hogg . . . by an old dissector* (Edinburgh, 1832), p. 17.

10 Anonymous review, 'Hogg's *Three Perils of Woman*,' *Emmet*, 18 Oct., 1823, pp. 25, 26.

11 James Hogg, *The Spy: A Periodical Paper of Literary Amusement and Instruction*, 24 Aug., 1811, p. 409.

12 Hogg, 'Memoir of the Author's Life,' pp. 80-81.

13 Douglas Gifford, *James Hogg* (Edinburgh, 1976), p. 72.

14 Browne, *The 'Life' of the Ettrick Shepherd Anatomized*, pp. 40, 48, 39.

15 Anon., 'Familiar Epistles to Christopher North, *From an Old Friend with a New Face*: Letter I: On Hogg's

Memoirs,' *Blackwood's Edinburgh Magazine*, Aug. 1821, pp. 44–45.

16 Browne, *The 'Life' of the Ettrick Shepherd Anatomized*, p. 6.

17 Anon. review, 'Hogg's *Tales*, &c.,' *Blackwood's Edinburgh Magazine*, May 1820, pp. 149, 148.

18 Hogg, 'Memoir of the Author's Life,' p. 54.

19 Anon., 'On the State of the Scotch Peasantry," *Scots Magazine*, Sept. 1800, pp. 484–488.

20 Anon. review, '*Lay Sermons*: by the Ettrick Shepherd,' *Fraser's Magazine*, July 1834, p.1.

21 Frye, *A Study of English Romanticism* (Chicago, 1968), p. 45.

22 Jean-Paul Sartre, *Existentialism and Humanism*, trans. Philip Mairet (London, 1948), pp. 55, 28.

23 Anon. review, 'The Annuals for 1828,' *La Belle Assemblée; or Court and Fashionable Magazine*, Nov. 1827, pp. 189–207.

24 James Hogg, letter to Frederick Shoberl, 2 Mar., 1833, in the National Library of Scotland, MS 1809, f. 184. I am grateful to Dr. Douglas S. Mack of Stirling University for drawing this letter to my attention, and to the Trustees of the National Library of Scotland for permission to quote from it.

25 *Quarterly Journal of Agriculture*, Aug. 1829, pp. 641, 640.

26 Hogg, 'Memoir of the Author's Life,' p. 14.

27 Hogg, letter to Frederick Shoberl, 2 Mar., 1833.

28 John Grieve, 'a hat manufacturer in Edinburgh,' also 'wrote highly creditable verses, but he is mainly to be remembered for the extensive patronage which he bestowed on many suffering men of letters' (editor's footnote, in Hogg's 'Memoir of the Author's Life,' *The Poetical Works of the Ettrick Shepherd*, 5 vols. (Glasgow, 1852), V, xxii).

29 Sir George Douglas, *James Hogg* (Edinburgh, 1899), p. 102, and Douglas Gifford, *James Hogg*, p. 235.

30 This description of Hogg's style is attributed to Walter Scott, in conversation with James Hogg, in Hogg's *Anecdotes of Sir W. Scott*, ed. Douglas S. Mack (Edinburgh, 1983), p. 43.

31 Hogg, 'Memoir of the Author's Life,' p. 46. The Shepherd's deep distrust of 'collegiate honours' and the 'walks of learning' sheds considerable light on the ironies of his 'Singular Dream,' 'First Sermon,' and 'Scottish Haymakers' — all of which depict 'collegians' and graduates in ways that at first seem flattering.

GLOSSARY

The following is a list of Scots words, and a few English words, which may give difficulty. It does not include simple words that have been spelled phonetically, or words which could be easily guessed by the reader.

a, a': all
ae: one
ahint: behind
ain: own
aince: once
airy: showy, conceited
an: if
ane: one
asteer: bustling, astir
auld: old
ava: at all, of all
aw: all
awa: away
aye: yes; still; ever; also
backbraid: a fall on the back
backsprent: the backbone
bairn: a child
Bashan: an ancient kingdom conquered by Moses, and noted for its stubborn bulls
bate: to reduce the expense
bauchle: a laughing-stock
beane: a bone; bean; (possibly) the lucky person who receives that piece of cake in which a bean has been hidden as a prize
beast: to beat, vanquish
beaver: a hat made from beaver fur
bedgown: a woman's working jacket
bellandine: a broil
bell-metal: hardened metal for making bells

belt bursten: beaten breathless
bent: coarse grass
benty-kneckit: bent-necked
biggin: a house, building
bire: a cowhouse
birk: a birch
birns: branches of heather
bit: small; a place
blink: a glimpse
blithemeat: food, usually bread and cheese,
  traditionally eaten to celebrate the birth of a child
bode: a potent; a bid; an invitation
body: a person
bogle: a ghost, apparition
boonmost: uppermost
bouet: a lantern
brank: a type of halter
branks: a bridle
braw: fine, handsome, good
breechin: a leather strap round the breach of a horse
breeks: trousers
buckling-comb: a clasp for fastening the hair
bung: the instep (of a shoe)
burked: to be smothered to death, then sold to
  medical men for dissection
burn: a brook
cambric: expensive white linen
canny: shrewd; skilful in midwifery; cannot
cantrips: magic, tricks
card: to prepare the wool for spinning
carl: a man; an old man
certes, certy: certainly; truth
chack: to catch between the teeth
chap: to strike; agree; call someone out by knocking
  on the window
choice: to choose
choppin: a quart
claut: a handful
claverin: chatting, gossipping

cleuch: a ravine, glen
clink: money
clippit: clipped, shorn
clout: a cloth; to repair
clouting: a beating
coft: bought
collegians: graduates or members of a college
corky-headit: giddy
corn: to feed with oats
coup: to overthrow
cour: to crouch
cowe: a bush; to cut, prune
crack: a story, lie, conversation; to chat; boast;
    become bankrupt
craim: a merchant's booth
crap: to creep
craw: a rook, crow; to brag
crock: an old ewe
cwotty (cutty): short
dadd: a blow; to strike
deil: devil
deil a bit: nothing at all, not at all
demity, dimity: fancy woven cotton
dike: a wall (usually of stone or peat)
dike-head: a wall dividing the pasture of a farm from
    the heather
ding: to overcome, beat, excel
dinna, disnae: do not
doit: a copper coin; a trifle
douce, douse: gentle, sweet, sober
dow: a dove
draff: dregs
draught: a drink
dud: a hare; a timorous person
duds: clothing
dugan: a poor weak fellow
edder: an adder
ee, e'e: the eye
een: eyes

eggler: someone who buys eggs from farmers and
　sells them at markets
eild: old
eneuch: enough
eyne: eyes
fairing: a present bought at a fair
faith (a mild oath): in faith
fash: to vex, trouble
fit: the foot
flack the breechin: to hesitate, hang back
fleechin: flattery
fock, focks: people
forret: forward
forty-five: the Jacobite rebellion of 1745
frae: from
fraebout: from about
gang: go
gar: to make, cause, compel
gart: to have caused, compelled
gate: way, manner
gaun: going
gawky: a bumpkin, simpleton
gayan: pretty much; middling
gear: clothes; property
geate: gate
gieing: giving
gin: if
Glauber's salts: sulfate of sodium
gliff: a moment
gloaming: the evening twilight
gluff: a scare, surprise
glyde: an old horse
gollaring: gurgling
goodman: the male head of a house; a husband;
　a tenant-farmer
goodwife: the mistress of a house; a wife
gouk: a fool; the cuckoo
grave-pole: a heavy, wooden pole
grit: great

grue: to shudder; to creep
guid: good; God
guidit: handled, used
haffats: locks of hair, especially hair hanging from the temples
haggy: broken
hale: whole; health
half-seas-over: tipsy
hallan: a wall in a cottage, usually between the door and the chimney
hamel: homely, plain
harrigalds: locks of hair; intestines
haud: to hold; a hold
haver: to talk idly
headsteel: the front of a bridle
hempy: a wild young rogue
herdit: herded the sheep
herns: brains
hie: to go quickly
hind: a farm-servant
hogg: a young sheep
houdy: a midwife
hough: the leg
hout fie: for shame!
howe: a hollow; glen; the middle
hye: to go quickly
ilk, ilka: each
ill-faurd: unhealthy, unattractive
jalouse: to guess, imagine
Johnny Cope: a popular Scottish Jacobite song; a nick-name for a rifle
kail: a kind of cabbage
kail-yard: a kitchen garden
ken: to know
kend: known; knew
kerlin, kerling: an old woman
kimmer: a gossip; midwife
kirk: a church
lair: a bed

lammie: a young lamb
laudanum: opium in solution
lave: the rest
laverack, laverock: a lark
lift: the sky
linn: a precipice over which water flows
lootching: lurching
lug: the ear
lumb: a chimney
mair: more
married on: married to
marrow: a lover; an equal
maun, mawn: must
mauna, maunna: must not
mell: to mix, be intimate; join battle
mense: honour, sense
messan: a small dog (or person)
meynde: to remember, mind
mickle, miekle: great
minnie: mother
muckil, muckle: much, great
mugg: a kind of sheep noted for its wool
muir: a moor
nain kind: own kind
neb: the nose
noor: not
nor: than
Od (a mild oath): God
ony: any
or: before
ower, owre: over
oxter: the arm, armpit; breast
paulie: a feeble lamb; runt
pawky: shrewd, sly
peat-knowe: a mound of peats
phiz: a beard; face
phrenology: a science, once very popular in Edinburgh,
   which estimated a person's abilities and disposition
   by examining his or her skull.

pike: to pick

pingle: to struggle

polled: beheaded (after Edinburgh criminals were hanged, their heads were often taken off and given to medical professors for demonstration and experimentation)

post-chaise: a travelling carriage for hire

poust: strength

poyet: a poet

precentor: the person who leads the congregation in singing

press: a cupboard

rad, *rade*: to fear; fear

reprobate: an outcast from salvation

saft: pleasant; weak; effeminate; half-witted

sair: sore, sad

Sandy: a nickname for a Scotsman

sanna: shall not

sarsnet: fine silk

sauf: to save

saul: the soul

saunna: shall not

saur: a savour, odour

sel o' her: herself

sel o' him: himself

sen: since

sennin: a sinew

sheep-drain: a ditch or pipe for draining pasture

sheil: a hut for shepherds

shilpit: pale

shoon: shoes

sic, siccan, sickan, sik: such

sin: since

skelp: to whip, beat, hammer

skelpie: a mischievous girl

skerr: a ridge

skype: a worthless fellow

slooch: anything contemptible; an idle fellow

smack: a kiss; a bang (from a gun)

smashis: big, burly; a strong person

smearing-house: a hut for tarring sheep

snibbelt: a piece of wood used in a tether

spain: to wean

spaulds: limbs

spear, speer: to ask

stand the lane o' him: stand by himself

stap: to stuff

steck: stack

steelity here, steelity there: whatever may happen; regardless

steer: to move, stir

stern: a star

stock: the front part of a bed

stool of repentance: a seat in church on which miscreants had to do public penance

strod: to stride, walk

strow: a quarrel, turmoil

sunks: a cushion or saddle

supple: limp

swee: to swing; a swing or inclination to one side

sweyer (sware): a level place between two hills

taickle: wrestling; a contract; punishment

tatty: rough, matted

tauk: to talk

tawpie: a blockhead; a foolish girl

the night: this night

thief: Satan

thrapple: the windpipe; neck

thraw: to throw

till: to

timmer: wooden

tint: to lose; lost

tippling: drinking

tod: a fox

toddy: a hot drink composed of whisky, water, and sugar

touzle, towzle: to toss hay; ruffle

traces: a harness made of straps or chains

troth: truth
trow: to feel certain
tup: a ram
twa, twae: two
twote: the sum
uncanny: unearthly, ghostly, supernatural; awkward; imprudent
unco: very
uphaud: to uphold, maintain
wad: would; to marry
walth: wealth
warstle: to wrestle
wat: to know
wauffest: weakest
waur: worse; goods
wean: an infant
wedder: an unsexed ram
weel: well
ween: to boast; an infant
whalp: a whelp
wheen: number, quantity, group of
whilk: which
wight: strong, stout; a fellow
willy-whand: a willow wand
winna: will not
woar: worse
won: to dwell; obtain; drying (hay)
wont: accustomed
wordie: word, oath
wot: to know
wother: a small weight added to offset the wrapping or vessel in which goods are sold
yaud: an old horse or cow
yeance, yeans: once
yince: once
yoke: to join, match, wrestle
yowe: a ewe